"Each of Michael C. Keith's pieces of micro-fictions lingers like an amuse-bouche on the palate of the intellect. With only a few words Keith's sketches set our anxieties, neuroses, and fears dancing like hobgoblins. And while we may marvel, even laugh, at the ingenuity of his observations, we are haunted by their familiarity and insightfulness." —*Michigan Quarterly Review*

"Michael C. Keith is a panopticon, scanning our contradictory relationships, language, and lives (as well as his own) for their follies. In *Pieces of Bones and Rags*, his fourth recent collection of one page, one paragraph, or one-sentence stories, he proves a master satirist."
—DeWitt Henry, founding editor of Ploughshares and author of *Sweet Marjoram*

"What Michael C. Keith has created here with these masterful micro-fictions is a kind of literary equivalent of an illuminated manuscript. And what he illuminates, measure by measure, is nothing short of the complex gear works of humankind: the light-hearted, meditative, quirky, and profound pared down record of our doings—stunningly unique, yet universal to us all."
—Robert Scotellaro, author of *What Are the Chances?* and *Nothing Is Ever One Thing*

PIECES OF BONES AND RAGS

Michael C. Keith

CATLETT, VA

PIECES OF BONES AND RAGS
Copyright © 2021 Michael C. Keith

ISBN: 978-1-7348324-6-4

First paperback edition published by Cabal Books
JUNE 2021

Published in the United States by Cabal Books.

The characters and events in this book are fictitious. Any similarity to real persons, living or dead, is coincidental and not intended by the author.

www.cabalbooks.us

Book Design by Michael Kazepis
Cover Artwork by Susanne Riette

CABAL BOOKS
DBA Thicke & Vaney Books
P. O. Box 223
Catlett, VA 20119

What is in the marrow is hard to take out of the bone.
IRISH PROVERB

Love is the rags of time.
JOHN DONNE

How much of this stuff is just plain chop-chop?
BILLY ROSEWATER

BEASTLY THOUGHTS

I'm thinking maybe my dog is acting strange because she knows I'm losing my mind. She senses my breakdown and is frightened for both of us. If I end up in the looney bin, where will she end up? There's no one who'll take her in. She has intuited our disaster. What a burden, her perception.

THE CURIOUS ACT OF A STRANGER LONG AGO

"I can see myself in the glass," said the child staring at the display window of Pettigrew & Stephens on Sauchiehall Street in Glasgow just before I stole her away.

It was that which was written on a postcard dated April 12, 1904 and found tucked into page 103 of Claude Bernard's *An Introduction to the Study of Experimental Medicine* in Paris's *Bibliotheque de la Sorbonne.*

Siren Stomach

There'd been so many air raid bombings on our village because of the RAF base nearby that the local apothecary ran out of Dinneford's Pure Fluid Magnesia. In its absence, we were left to suffer our dyspepsia, indigestion, flatulence, and torpidity of the liver. Our hatred of the bloody Huns provided some small relief.

Good Grief

He felt guilty because he experienced a certain pleasure in his mother-in-law's failing health. She was a decent enough woman, but he'd never felt genuinely close to her because of her conservative values. In politics and religion, she was an old-school right-winger through and through. Now, she was battling a serious heart issue, which was to be addressed with a risky surgical procedure, and he half hoped she wouldn't survive. *What an inhumane and compassionless attitude*, he told himself. When she came through the surgery in flying colors, everyone was happy, and he tried to appear equally cheerful. But it took no small effort to hide his disappointment. A few days later the elderly woman died from a stroke and while he didn't feel particularly buoyant about her passing, there was an undeniable gladness in his soul.

THESE TIMES

Eighteen-year-old Silas Birch felt he was cursed to be living at a point in history when there was so much uncertainty. "It isn't fair," he grumbled when his mother informed him that the college he was scheduled to attend was likely to cancel its fall semester because of the pandemic. "Why?" he growled. "It only kills *old* people." Silas was beginning to hate his grandparents.

What He Told His Son on His Away Bed

"I find the word 'dead' deplorable . . . an insult to the deceased. 'He's dead' is like saying he's nothing. Worse, it's like saying he's refuse . . . just a disposable *thing*. Not even a recyclable. What a disgusting way to refer to someone who has lived a full life. Someone who did good things. Someone who loved and was loved in return. You let anyone call me *dead*, and I'll come back to haunt you. Tell them I'm away. Yes, *away* is better."

What Remains

Sam Barclay had spent four years in a French prison for involuntary manslaughter. He'd come to the defense of a women being attacked by a man in a café and his act of chivalry caused the assailant to strike his head against the leg of a wrought iron table. The deceased turned out to be the woman's husband, and Barclay was viewed as a meddler in a lover's quarrel. The court had little sympathy for such intervention, especially by a foreigner. When the American finished his sentence, he quickly left Paris, returning to his home in Akron, Ohio. By then he'd become something of a hero to the local population, which believed his gallant deed had been woefully handled by the French legal system. However, despite his unfortunate experience abroad, Barclay still held French wine in high regard.

THE GIFT OF NONCHALANCE

He climbed into his car and immediately noticed the passenger side door was missing. He didn't make much of it, reminding himself he had no passenger with him.

POSEYVILLE, INDIANA, 1953

Our house was at the far edge of town on a gravel road that came to an end at the creek we spent most of every summer fishing. Because we hardly ever caught anything in it, it didn't attract other folks. That was fine with Pa, because he couldn't abide strangers or even people he knew, for that matter. In fact, it seemed he just barely tolerated us, although Ma treated him like he was the nicest person there was. It's not that he wasn't okay with me and my younger brother. It's just that he never stopped telling us he had hidden a gun somewhere close by and he knew how to use it. He would say that out of the blue when we sat with him on the porch or worked the fields with him. Blurt it out like there was someone else there with us. It didn't seem like it was intended for us, but it didn't seem like it wasn't. My little brother would ask me about it, but I didn't have an explanation. Finally, we just accepted there was a gun hidden somewhere on the property, and it was important to Pa that we knew it.

A SAMPLE OF HOW THE PASSAGE OF TIME INFLUENCES EVERYTHING

She traded her yellow for blue but then realized what she really wanted was purple. Still, she felt blue suited her more than yellow. It took her years to finally find someone willing to swap their purple for her blue, but by then purple just didn't seem right for someone her age.

Company

It was on the twentieth anniversary of his owning the house that Justin first noticed the breathing sound—someone or something inhaling and exhaling. At first, he thought it might be the wind and then figured it was likely an animal inside the walls of the old structure. He quickly discounted both theories because of the human quality of the noise. Yet it made no sense because he was the only one residing in the rambling Victorian. The steady cadence was undeniably there, however, and he attempted to pin down its location, moving from room to room. Without solving the puzzle, he finally held his own breath thinking it may be what he was actually hearing, but the airy emissions continued. Eventually, he concluded there was a ghost living with him, probably a person who'd died in the house a century ago, and he felt okay with that. He'd been lonely too long.

When You Find Your Reality in Fiction

Well, there I am, he thought, reading the first two sentences in a Lydia Davis short story, called "In a Northern Country." *Five years beyond my seventieth with a sciatic leg and asthmatic lung.*

The Benefits of Knowing Your Body

I never learned to breathe from the diaphragm, so I was never much of an announcer, although I worked as one the better part of a decade. In other words, I spent ten years doing something I could never be really good at. I think back now and wonder what my life would have been, at least professionally, if I had known how to get the most out of my voice box.

LOOKING FOR AMERICA

Back in the 80s, Craig and his new wife traveled west on their honeymoon. He'd just read Dee Brown's *Bury My Heart at Wounded Knee* and wanted to take the opportunity to visit the site where the subject of the book unfolds. The young couple drove from the northern part of the Pine Ridge Indian Reservation that reaches to Interstate 90 and after two dusty hours on a gravel road came upon the place where 300 hundred Lakota Sioux, mostly women and children, were massacred by the U.S. Cavalry. Expecting to encounter a shiny tourist pavilion like the one they'd just seen at Mt. Rushmore, they were surprised to find a rusty lean-to, crumbling shed, and graffitied historical marker that told of the slaughter in broken English. They were indignant that something more fitting hadn't been erected by the government to commemorate such a tragic event in American history. When they asked a passing tribal elder about it, he replied, "Would Jews have let Hitler build them a shrine?"

And He Replied . . .

"I'm having my Sunday morning screaming fantods."

She left the kitchen without saying another word for she knew there would be knife throwing.

Immaculate Conception Two

She grew flowers from her vagina at a time when other girls were experiencing their first periods. A spray of fairy foxglove and forget-me-nots had sprung from her lap. She believed she was having her first menstruation, since no one had told her what to expect. The following month, to her joy and further puzzlement, a lovely baby's breath appeared.

An Eye for Detail

All of the stone walls in Bedfordshire had been dismantled and scattered about. When Chief Constable Davis discovered one stone was missing, concern grew.

OLD GUY DANCING

When Clarence picked up on the Starland Vocal Band's hit, "Afternoon Delight," while he was in the soup aisle at the Stop & Shop he couldn't keep himself from cutting a move. He waved his arms high and strutted around his shopping cart as two teenage girls looked on with extreme amusement. When he caught sight of them, he pointed to the region below his belt and quipped, "My sky rockets in flight." The girls laughed hysterically, flipped their tiny skirts upward, and skittered away. The senior shopper was full of appreciation.

WHAT KIND OF A DAY IS THIS?

There's an ambulance at the Dollar Tree. A dead man inside. He's 42 and the father of three. There to buy something for his daughter. "A heart attack," says the EMT to the horrified store manager, Winifred Cummings. "He was looking for these," she mumbles, holding a bag labeled Mia Tonytail Wraps.

Adjusting to One's Surroundings

Rattlesnakes were everywhere on the mesa, and she was terrified of running into one. She moved gingerly along the narrow dirt path and every couple of steps she stamped her feet because she'd heard that the noise and vibrations would scare the reptiles into hiding. When she got back to her friend's house where she was staying for the week she was told that if you got near a rattler and stomped the ground it would likely strike at you out of fear it was being attacked. From that point on, she would only venture into the wild when there were tires under her.

DIGGING HIS GRAVE

Because I defended Barry Manilow when my friends made a joke about him, they now shun me. *They just don't get it,* I thought. "Hey, I like the Beatles, too. 'I Want to Hold Your Hand' is magic."

Breaking Bread Together

It was an eye-opener to Rhea when she realized she was never actually hungry and that she only ate because it was expected—breakfast, lunch, supper. So, she stopped eating because the clock said it was time to do so. Things were fine initially, and then she realized not eating when everyone else was eating made her lonely. Now, she eats when she needs the company.

LIFE GOES ON

In 1949, little Jamie Colman was diagnosed with leukemia and sent to Children's Hospital in Boston. He was carefully examined and transfused in the Hematology and Oncology Department. Doctors there told his parents there was nothing more that could be done for their child and they should make the most of his remaining days. Jamie's condition rapidly worsened over the next few weeks, and Mr. and Mrs. Colman prepared as best they could for their nine-year-old's imminent demise. The bleak situation had taken a toll on the enthusiasm they had shared for their long-planned Caribbean vacation, but they nonetheless fixed the date of departure and hoped it wouldn't have to be rescheduled.

IMPROVISATION

The elderly woman in black shuffles about her dusty courtyard and spots a rattlesnake coiled up next to a mesquite bush. Instead of sticking it to death or brooming it away as she usually does, she grabs the canvas she's been working on intending to add the reptile and curses as it slithers into a hole at the base of the adobe wall. Undeterred, she applies a squiggly streak of ochre, steps back, and nods approvingly.

GRASPING THE MATTER

If his mom fed him Cream of Wheat for breakfast one more time, Dondi vowed to attack her with the butter knife. It had reached that desperate point for the nine-year-old. He'd complained to her countless times that the cereal made him gag, but she continued to serve it to him. When she wasn't looking he sometimes dumped the steaming cement-colored gruel into the trash, but she'd become more and more suspicious of him and often hung around the kitchen until he begrudgingly emptied his bowl. Finally, the "one more time" came, and when his parent put the dreaded porridge in front of him he grabbed the spreader and slathered butter all over her arm. Although shocked, she finally got it. *Yes,* she thought, *he's trying to tell me that he'd prefer his Cream of Wheat* not *be heated*

WHEN STUFF GOES MISSING

The things he went looking for weren't there, and that terrified him. Just that morning he'd searched for milk in the refrigerator and couldn't find it. When he reported this to his wife, she pointed to a full container on the top shelf. His heart dropped. Just the day before he couldn't find his car in the driveway.

Outside Looking In

The new kid who moved into the neighborhood with his family was our age but much bigger than the rest of the kids who lived there. He didn't smile much either, so we were a little afraid of him. We figured he could beat us up if he wanted to, and he kind of looked like he wanted to. He would stand on his porch and watch us play but we would ignore him, figuring it was better to keep our distance. When my mom asked why we didn't include him in our games, I just told her he didn't seem interested in what we were doing. "You have to make an effort with him," she said, adding, "He has a developmental disorder that makes him more withdrawn than other kids." She didn't explain what that meant, and when I told my friends what she said, we figured he really was dangerous.

Soldier's Scrapbook

"What I recall most about the people who lived in the tiny village outside my army base in Korea was their blank expressions—they didn't smile or nothing—and, oh yeah, how they would crouch on their haunches when talking with each other. Made my legs ache just looking at them. 'Course, I never knew any of the locals. Didn't try. They were different, so I wasn't interested. I was just there because of the war."

LATENT MARGAUX

She doesn't like the concert. It isn't her thing, she says. Why didn't she say that when I told her I was going to buy us tickets? They cost a frigging fortune, and now she's sitting here looking bored while one of the best groups ever performs. This is why I should break up with her. She does this all the time. At the restaurant yesterday, she says she's not big on Italian food, even though she said nothing until we were looking at the menus. The same at the movie last week when halfway through it she remarks she knew she wasn't going to like it. It wasn't her kind of story. Oh, yeah, and we're in the Caribbean a couple months ago and she informs me she prefers snow over sand. That the beach makes her itchy and gives her a rash. Six-grand for a bad time. No, we're through. This relationship isn't working. I ask her if she thinks we should separate, and she nods okay. I don't even want to think what she's going to say when I start packing.

Give Them What They Want

Viewers were provided the option of two endings. Producers acted on critic's comments that their film was anti-climactic and generally unsatisfying. The war drama featured two long time adversaries trading swords for ploughshares. The new ending had the battling armies slaughtering one another. Surveys of ticketholders showed that bloodshed trumped peaceful resolution by a 100 to 1 margin, once again confirming the dissolute tastes of the American public. Of course, an even more savage sequel was planned based on the movie's tremendous box office success.

An Etymologist Is Born

Isn't Powder River like saying steel clouds? Horace mused, examining a map of Wyoming. *Word combinations . . . man, they're the world's great mystery.* It was then he realized where his young life was now going to take him.

Eco-Terrorist

Litter kept mounting up on his street, and it really upset him. From his perspective, it reflected the indifference of his neighbors toward the environment and the general appearance of the place in which they lived. Things suddenly took a darker turn when a Dunkin Donuts opened a block away. The amount of trash strewn about from passing cars grew exponentially. Still his fellow homeowners did nothing to address what he saw as a growing blight. *What kind of people live here*, he wondered, his anger rising. Finally, out of desperation, he removed the accumulated refuse himself, filling several jumbo plastic bags. He then barricaded the street with them and when drivers climbed from their cars to clear their path, he'd curse them and pelt them with their own rubbish. He did not regard this as over the top behavior.

A Question Arose as to the Translator's Credibility

"The first draft of Matsuo Basho's most famous haiku was: 'A dull murky lake . . . A cart falls into the lake, boom!' It bears little resemblance to the final version: "An old silent pond . . . A frog jumps into the pond, splash!'"

TRAPPED IN THE ETHEREAL

Among the two-dozen vintage radios he owned the one he favored most was his table model Crosley 817. He remembered the day his father first brought it into the house over 70 years ago. What continued to please him about the old set was that it played the same program he first heard on it. No matter how many times he listened to it, he never grew tired of following the strange incident that occurred near Grover's Mill—just down the road from where he lived. It also intrigued him that every time he turned on the antique receiver the night time sky would turn a bright crimson.

Infinite Degrees of Separation

A Supermarine Spitfire Vc 'Tropical' JK707 MX-P serving with the 307th Fighter Squadron, 31st Fighter Group operated by the 12th USAAF carries Jonathan Lebarge to his death in North Africa on the day his mother back in Boone, North Carolina, excitedly shows her best friend the letter she just received from him declaring he'll be home soon.

The 18ᵗʰ Century Was Not Kind to Young Laborers

The master chimney sweep greased up 11-year-old Emil Percival's gaunt body for his ascent up the dark innards of the brick and mortar stack. It was the third time this was done that day, and the child had lost the enthusiasm and energy he'd had for the sixpence he was promised after performing three to four such tasks in a day. "You clean it good, boy, you hear, and do it fast or I'll light a fire under your feet. We got another to go," said the head man. "Yes, sir," replied the boy meekly, as he burrowed into the narrow aperture. The process involved moving up the stack as far as elbowing and squirming would take you and removing the soot from the blocks with a brush and metal scraper. Emil's small frame was built for the chore but his strength had been drained and when he reached as far as he could, he lost consciousness. His weak heart had stopped from the shortage of air in the flue and extreme malnutrition he suffered his whole life. "How's it going, lad?" inquired the boss sweeper, tugging at the rope secured about the youngster's waist 60 feet above. When no answer came, he repeated his question and again pulled at the noose. "You deaf, boy?" he shouted, this time yanking hard at the line. When there still was no answer, an upsetting thought occurred to him, *Shite, this be the second climbing boy this month I lost and, look here, my rum flask be empty.*

EEK!

Her manuscript of verse had been waiting publication for a year and now the launch day was almost at hand. During the period leading up to its release, she would frequently review the small volume and each time her confidence in its quality grew. It was the week before its debut she perceived a major flaw in its contents. To her horror it appeared to lack a single instance of onomatopoeia.

THE POWER OF FILM

Allen Halper wanted to be a cowboy since growing up in Queens, New York. He'd spent endless hours in smoky movie houses watching westerns, and he thought the cowboy's life the most wonderful and exciting of anything an adult could do. He did not want to join his father's hosiery manufacturing company, nor did he want to waste his time going to the business college his father attended. So, upon graduating high school, he packed his suitcase, emptied his savings account, and set out for the west, where he planned to look for a job as a ranch hand. He targeted Oakley, Kansas, as a good place to start his search for no other reason than it had been a scene location for a cattle drive in a movie starring Randolph Scott. He figured someone in town could tell him who was hiring. After downing a burger at The Bluff, he made his inquiry and was told the Circle K off Service Road 31 was looking for experienced help. He took a local conveyance to the site and was hired on the spot after telling the foreman he'd been "punching cows" since he was 12. In no time at all he was able to mount a horse.

Fruits of War

There's a small indentation in the identification tag GIs are issued when they enter the military. The one-inch piece of stainless-steel hangs around the soldier's neck on a chain like a St. Christopher's medal. A medic positions the slot between the troop's front teeth when he's killed in battle and gives his jaw a good thump, driving the dog tag between his incisors so it won't fall out when his body is in transit back home. A practical design, if there ever was one.

How Statistics Make a Difference

Jess told Ron that over a hundred people die every year from falling tree branches. When Ron heard that he felt his lifelong deep-rooted suspicion of trees was justified. "I been keeping away from forests and parks since I was a little kid," he proudly declared.

When Fate Works in Your Behalf and Less So in Behalf of Others

The flat at 6 Melina Place in the Borough of St. Marglebone was much more luxurious than he was accustomed to. Its advertisement in the *Evening Standard* had attracted his eye because of its unusually low rent and stately address. He was dubious about its actual availability but inquired just the same. Sure enough, he found he could afford the rooms and enthusiastically thanked the owner of the baronial manse for letting them to him. Later, as he was nestled under the down comforters of the four-poster canopy bed, he felt a modicum of guilt for having taken advantage of the landlord, who was clearly in the grips of a brain fever of the type often afflicting the very elderly. Despite this, he slept extravagantly.

GOING HOLLYWOOD

Hugh Wystan spent his life writing poetry in obscurity. Publishing his work didn't interest him. The process of creating verse did. When his friend, also a poet, published his first collection of poetry and gained critical attention, Wystan was happy for him, although he was perplexed as to why his fellow scribe suddenly let his hair grow long, sported an ascot, and took up a pipe.

EVIDENTIARY

From the street, her camera caught the silhouette of a man's upper body through the second level window of Fisherman's Grotto. It was 1962 and subsequent Kodak Brownie photos at the scene revealed it was my father dining with his girlfriend, the one my mother later told me about. She said she'd followed him to the restaurant and confronted him and his lover there. He'd denied having an affair with the much younger woman, but she knew better. The pictures were used in the divorce trial. I never saw my father again. He'd moved to the East Coast with his new wife. One night, I crushed the camera to smithereens with my Louisville Slugger.

Red Skins

She saw her first Native American in a country and western bar in Cody, Wyoming, while on a road trip to Yellowstone and was very excited. He wasn't exactly like the Indians in movies or on TV. She'd seen his shirt at Macy's when shopping for a birthday gift for her husband. *I suppose that makes sense these days*, she told herself. Still, it detracted from her image of what indigenous people should look like.

Second Thoughts

His daily pill dispenser indicated it was Thursday. He was convinced it was Saturday and that he'd apparently forgotten to take his meds for two days. To make up for this oversight, he took the backlog of capsules as well as those for the current day. He later realized it was, in fact, Thursday, and he wondered what effect the overdose might have on him. In the first hour, he felt fine, but a while later he began to notice a rapid heartbeat. He called his estranged wife for advice, and she recommended he come to her apartment so she could keep an eye on him. He thought it was kind of her to suggest that, since she herself was dealing with the effects of the poison he'd slipped into the cocoa he'd given her. *Maybe I've been too harsh on her*, he thought. *No, I'll bring over some more Hershey's.*

FUN AT THE BALLPARK

Brass Knuckles Night was this year's annual fan event and expectations were high. Last year's number of severe wounds at Switchblade Night had been disappointing,

Street Lady

Malina had worn holes in the bottoms of her shoes following Rodavan wherever he went in Vrsac. She feared if she didn't keep him in constant view, she may never see him again. That horrified her, because she was desperately in love with him, although he did not know it. If he did, he'd have her arrested for stalking him. It would not go well for her, since she'd obsessively shadowed many other men throughout her life. *Have I harmed anyone yet? Why won't they just leave me alone to do what is in my heart?* she wondered.

Non-Life-Threatening Injuries

The car plunged off the towering cliff at a high-rate of speed slamming against rocks and coming to rest in 50 feet of water. Rescuers managed to locate the driver an hour later and removed her from the wreckage. After she was released from the hospital later in the day, having suffered only minor scratches and bruises, everyone in town recognized the recently arrived Venutian possessed a hardier constitution than Earthlings.

DYING HIGH

Dozens of construction workers died in the 1930s while building New York City skyscrapers. Horace McCarthy was one of them. While several men saw him fall, his body was never recovered. Searches were conducted on the roofs of buildings below the point from which he'd toppled, but nothing was found. It was if he'd just evaporated. Rumors circulated that Horace had been hitting the bottle again and was inebriated when he lost his balance. His widow argued that her husband never took a drop of the spirits while on the job, but she was refuted by eyewitnesses, who reported Horace was doing the Irish jig on a freshly installed beam when he lost his footing. "Horace danced when he was sober, too," countered his spouse.

OTHERWORLDLY . . . IF YOU LET IT

When I stood up, I was a foot taller than when I'd sat down. My head was inside the chandelier and all the little glass diamonds that hung from it glinted in my eyes, blinding me. For a moment, I felt I was in danger, and then I thought, *what the hell, just go with it*, and I did. Neptune was incredible.

Child Welfare

Mark believed Blake, Nebraska, was a fine place to raise a nine-year-old, even if there was just him to do it—his wife had inexplicably vanished weeks before. There was no crime to speak of in the farming community, so a kid could wander all over without being in any particular danger. Of course, that was before he learned it had been declared the landing site for hostile aliens. When he got the news, it was too late for him to do much about it, except direct his son to go play outside, distracting the invaders enough to allow him to hide in the storm cellar. It was there he found his missing wife.

A Hiccup in the Hadron?

The sand in the hourglass stopped halfway as my eggs boiled. And when I looked out of the window, I saw a wave stalled mid-roll. Then I noticed my neighbor's skiff suspended in the air. *This is not going to be a normal day*, I thought.

Not All Imagined is Unreal

I know I'm a bit of a hypochondriac, and everyone pretty much thinks that, in particular my wife, who has lost patience with me. Thankfully, I can still complain about my latest medical concern with my two best friends, but I can tell they're also losing interest in hearing about my ills, which are not all fantasized. Just today I've been Googling about a sharp pain in my right buttock, and when I told them about it, to my satisfaction they agreed that it sounded like a real pain in the ass to them.

I'm Going to Die

No! No! No! No! No! No! No! No! No! No! No! No!
No! No! No! No! No! No! No! No! No! No! No! No!
No! No! No! No! No! No! No! No! No! No! No! No!
No! No! No! No! No! No! No! No! No! No! No! No!
No! No! No! No! No! No! No! No! No! No! No! No!
No! No! No! No! No! No! No! No! No! No! No! No!
No! No! No! No! No! No! No! No! No! No! No! No!
No! No! No! No! No! No! No! No! No! No! No! No!
No! No! No! No! No! No! No! No! No! No! No! No!
No! No! No! No! No! No! No! No! No! No! No! No!
No! No! No! No! No! No! No! No! No! No! No! No!
No! No! No! No! No! No! No! No! No! No! No! No!
No! No! No! No! No! No! No!! No! No! No!

....

Re-Runs

My Yellow Lab sleeps on the floor at the side of my bed, her paws thrashing about as the recording device in her head replays the desperate leaps of the rabbit she stalks during our morning hike to the pond. Growling, she nips at the carpet and has her victory.

Any Day You Can Solve a Mystery Is a Good Day

He found deep rutted wagon wheel tracks against a large boulder at the far edge of his 730-acre spread on the eastern plains of Wyoming. He'd bought the place just three months earlier and was still exploring parts of the property. This particular discovery intrigued him, because it looked as if the impressions came directly out from under the giant rock. *Impossible. How could that be?* he wondered. Upon further inspection, he noticed a set of tracks led up to the other side of the monolith. It was if the wagon had somehow burrowed under the rock and resurfaced on the other side. Or weirder still, had gone through it. Try as he might, he could not come up with a reasonable explanation. He did, however, determine why the carburetor on his 1953 Ford F100 was leaking.

It Was in His Nature

Clovis had his forehead pecked by a crow as he jogged the path that led to his cabin. It was the first time such a thing had happened and he was disillusioned by country living on the spot. *This sort of violence never happened to me when I lived in the city*, he thought, packing his things for a return to a more civilized environment.

0.5 MG, 1.0 MG, 1.5 MG, 2.0 MG

One Xanax calmed him. Two unruffled him. Three muddled him. Four removed him. His wife made certain she had enough on hand to provide him the relief *she* needed.

AND HOW DO YOU THINK THAT MADE US FEEL?

She could play the cello better than any of us, and while we admired her, we also envied her exceptional musicianship. She made us all sound unpracticed and even amateurish. We knew that wasn't intentional on her part. She was a very sincere and down-to-earth individual. It was just who she was—a virtuoso performer who should be playing in a more prestigious orchestra. We tried to convince her of that, but she insisted she was a long way from being ready. That made us feel even worse than we already did. What did that say about us? Eventually, we came to really resent her and went out of our way to make her time with us unpleasant. And then, out of the blue, she was offered a seat with a renowned symphony in Denver and we saw this as an opportunity to be rid of her. To our chagrin, she declined the offer. Now we were desperate to be free of this constant reminder of our subpar abilities. After several closed-door meetings, we decided on a course of action. Finally, we agreed there was only one thing left to do . . . ask her for music lessons.

LIVES OF THE PARTY

In his state of delirium, Porter imagined each part of a centipede cut into pieces could walk on its own. Later, when he was lucid, he tried it and found it was true. It intrigued him and at social gatherings he invariably brought along an arthropod and scalpel to impress people with his discovery.

MAN'S BEST FRIEND

Barry Ephram had to get out of bed or go crazy. The idea he was on the cusp of going bankrupt panicked him, and he knew if he didn't move he'd scream and wake his wife. He groped his way through the dark bedroom and down the stairs to the kitchen. Turning the light on helped lower his anxiety but not enough to keep him from pounding his fist against the refrigerator door. This roused his dog, who came running to him, tail wagging and leaping to lick him. "Hey, baby," he mumbled, ruffling the fur on the back of its neck. "Daddy's losing his mind. Going nuts. Should he shoot himself? Huh . . . should he?" It surprised Barry when his beloved pet barked in the affirmative. It'd always barked when it wanted something.

TIMOTHY, THE PRECOCIOUS 11-YEAR-OLD, ASKED . . .

"What's the sense of getting a tattoo when it disappears after you die? Same with body piercings?" he added. "Oh, and plastic surgery for that matter?"

LUCKY ADOPTION

When I laughed at the idea that the dog made the soup, it looked at me with a mix of anger and hurt in his large brown eyes. "Who else could have made it?" I thought I heard it say. The other morning a voice announced the coffee was ready, and when I entered the kitchen, there was the dog standing by the stove. There was no other human in the house, so I questioned whether it was possible it was him. Now with the steaming bowl of soup on the table I realized I had an exceptionally capable shelter dog.

Why Does There Always Have to Be a Downside

He had reached another level of insomnia. There was no more just being unable to fall asleep or waking up in the middle of the night not able to get back to sleep. Now he couldn't sleep at all. That wouldn't be so bad, he thought, if not sleeping didn't kill you, because he surely could put the extra time to good use.

STRONG OPINIONS

At first, I have laryngitis. Then a stuffy nose followed by a sore throat. Chills and aches set in next. A cold, I tell myself . . . maybe the flu. My father used to call it the grip. "You got the grip, son," he would say. My mom called it a virus. "You've probably come down with the virus thing that's been going around." I'm told by my friend it's a possible reaction to the seasonal flu shot I got over the weekend. "It can make you feel like you have the real thing," he says. My girlfriend says that's not likely. "Everyone I know who's had a reaction to the shot has the sweats and a high temp. You don't. All you have is a 24-hour bug." I go to bed, and in the morning, there's not a trace of it. I buy an engagement ring.

How Self-Image Can Turn on a Dime

Myron could migrate into other people's heads. He had no power to manipulate the minds he entered but he could fully explore their cognitive range and abilities. When on an impulse at the local Stop and Shop he decided to transfer into the brain of the developmentally disabled bag boy, his world was turned upside down. *Oh my God*, he thought, *he's so much smarter than I am.*

WEATHERING CHANGE

Thirty years back he'd bought a cottage on the shore just south of Chatham on the Cape. It was he and his wife's summer refuge and a place he always felt at ease. With climate change, it was threatened by rising seas and he anticipated it would be underwater in the not too distant future, perhaps five years. He'd done all he could to preserve the house by building stone walls, sand dunes, and vegetation barriers, but they'd failed as the storms increased in frequency and ferocity. Finally, he decided to abandon the beloved property and leave it to its inevitable fate. It was one of the most difficult decisions he'd ever made. Given that he'd stopped paying taxes on the parcel of land, the town had foreclosed on it, turning it into a public beach. Possessing fond memories of the location, he returned to it occasionally complaining each visit about the $20 parking fee and the unreliability of nature.

LITTLE BURR DIDN'T SEE IT COMING

He thought about what he would do if he could make himself invisible and then he discovered he actually could. Without going into details, let's just say it was after a powerful electrical storm . . . *really*. Now he wanted to put the newfound ability to good use. He contemplated an endless list of possibilities. However, the first thing he decided to do was run up on stage during a performance of "Hamilton" and kick Aaron in the nuts.

Oh, Yeah, That's Right . . .

A resounding crash drew her attention away from her phone conversation with her sister. "Mark!" she screamed and ran in the direction of her husband's den and the source of the jarring sound. What she found when she got there shook her to the core. A vast hole in the ceiling rose two levels to the open sky. "He went through there," she whimpered, "Oh, my God, straight up into the clouds!" A few seconds passed and then she was reminded of something pivotal to her understanding of what had just happened. *He did say he'd recently acquired certain powers.*

So, To Hell with It

He drafted a story, revised it, then cursed its lack of brilliance. "What am I to do?" he asked his wife. "Stop writing," she suggested. He had always respected her opinion.

FORETOLD

Mable Zendaya Carter spent the 40s, 50s, and 60s living in the black quarter of Charlottesville. She then died before reaching her prime, or knowing what it would have been like to be something other than a charwoman for one of the city's wealthiest white families. Her aunt knew Mabel had been deprived her glory, because she'd seen the young woman's fortune in the cookie at Fook Hing's House of Wonton, which predicted a future of great accomplishments.

THE HIGHER CANINE SOUL

Ulf was a German Shephard trained to contain and, if necessary, attack Jews. He was good at his job but had recently refused to charge a little girl who had strayed too close to the camp's perimeter fence. It was the first time the sentry dog had ignored a command, and his handler was at a loss to explain his behavior. Ulf was not at a loss to explain his behavior however. There was just no fucking way he was going to accost a small child.

Moments Like These

His girlfriend's jealous ex-husband struck him in the head with a blunt object and he was out cold. When he came to a few minutes later, he was in an ambulance and his new lady was seated next to him holding his hand. "Wha . . .?" was the only sound he could muster as the paramedics inserted an IV into his arm. "Don't talk," they instructed him, but his girlfriend filled him in. "My ex is in the ambulance behind us. Not in such good shape. I knew sooner or later I would have to use my super powers," she whispered into his ear. Just before drifting out of consciousness, he was certain he saw sparks fly from her eyes.

TOUCHED FROM THE GRAVE

His deceased son visited him in his dream and asked for a loan as he often did when alive. Perturbed, he asked the 36-year-old why he didn't have a job so he could support himself. "I'm dead, for chrissake! How am I supposed to do that?" Recognizing his boy had a valid point, he handed him a million dollars, figuring in dreams you can do things like that and hoping it would be enough to keep him away for the rest of the night.

A Case of Her

In the early 70s I was obsessed with Joni. Her luminous gray-blue eyes, shoulder-length golden locks, and sweet girl-woman's body held me spellbound. And when she sang, "The Last Time I saw Richard," I would reach the full apogee of my climax. It was to me she was singing. Who else with a name like Richard?

Highly Improbable

Why would someone leave a food delivery bag on my front lawn? wondered Mark. *Does it have to do with what happened yesterday with the teenage dirt biker? Maybe it's a prank and full of shit just waiting for me to kick it or open it?* Mark had been disturbed by the screaming of the scooter's engine throughout the day before, and he'd finally had enough. As the culprit approached, he'd flagged him to stop. "You're disturbing the peace of the whole neighborhood with that thing!" he'd yelled, trying to be heard over the squealing machine. "Tough!" replied the kid, flipping his middle finger at Mark as he sped off. "Asshole!" he'd yelled after him, as the delinquent disappeared around the corner. His irritation returned as he reflected on the incident. With some trepidation, he took a whiff of the bag and happily concluded it was filled with still-warm Chinese food. *Hmm, maybe it's a peace offering,* he thought, a smile washing the frown from his face.

HOW THINGS START

When he was a young boy, he tossed a rock through the neighbor's window, and he just stood there when the owner came running out. He wasn't frightened. In fact, he felt nothing, which is why he didn't run or hide. When the neighbor asked him who broke her window, he just shrugged. The neighbor looked around suspiciously and went back inside. *Stupid woman,* thought the boy. It was the beginning of his life of crime.

A Recalled Experience from His Hobo Childhood

"Did you know if you walk on hot pavement in your worn-out shoes day after day without changing your socks, the sweat from your feet turn the fabric into crusty shells when you get up in the morning. What you have to do then is bang them on the floor or bed post to soften them, and when they're on it feels like you're walking on pebbles until they get sweaty again."

Inside Advice

On the morning of her colonoscopy, Ella forgot to fast and had her usual full breakfast. As she was taking her last bite she remembered she was not to have any food. "Oh, my god, what shall I do!" she fretted. "They'll cancel my procedure, and I'll have to go through all of this again. I just can't swallow a gallon of that disgusting liquid anymore. It's so awful." Her husband suggested she go through with the appointment anyway. "They should be able to discern the difference between blueberry granola waffles and a polyp."

CRIMINAL INTENT OFTEN BACKFIRES

Was there a way he could rid himself of her without being caught? Most of the murders he'd heard about resulted in arrests, and as much as she made his life miserable, he didn't want to end up in prison for the remainder of his days. *Maybe I could get someone to do it . . . a professional*, he thought. *Yes, that was the answer*, he decided, and set about to locate someone to hire. He realized too late that posting the job on Facebook was a mistake.

It Was Just So Easy to Reboot

He couldn't recall the number of times he'd committed suicide. *At least nine*, he calculated. He was about to do it again, because he just didn't like the way things were going at the moment. Given his bent for self-destruction, he knew he was fortunate to exist at a time when instant re-embodiment was available.

Mixed Feelings

He was shocked by what had been taken from him. *What will I do without my mouth?* he pondered, while feeling a growing sense of awe for a thief who knew how to keep his victim quiet.

Exposed

For years I've thought back to the empty stretch of shoreline on the Chesapeake Bay where I had removed my swim trunks and dared my wife and another couple to go skinny dipping with me. I'd always been a pretty modest guy, so my unexpected behavior surprised me. For some inexplicable reason my inhibitions were gone that particular instant. My wife and friends didn't appear shocked by my sudden bold act. However, they made no effort to remove their own clothes. After a moment, they turned away as if having just noticed a passing sea gull and resumed their conversation. I stood there feeling more and more awkward, if not perverted, and then slipped my swimsuit back on and quietly sat down. No one's ever mentioned what I did that day, and I'm thankful for that, but sometimes I think they're looking at me funny.

A REAL WINNER

We had more groceries than we could imagine. Bags and bags kept being unloaded in the kitchen. We were always hungry and our cupboards were empty most of the time because of our routinely jobless alcoholic father. My younger sisters and I were thrilled by what seemed a sudden and wonderful change of fortune. *Had he turned over a new leaf?* I speculated, suggesting he may actually have been working. "No," said our long-suffering mother. "He won the food raffle at the bar."

He Thought It Best for His Sanity to Leave Her

He claimed she kept everything bottled up inside and it caused him real problems. "I never know what's bothering you, what you're thinking. I can just tell from your expression that you're not happy." After a long pause, she replied, "What do you want me to say?"

TIPPING POINT

The Johnsons had three children, all academic overachievers with exceptional IQs. Their parents were well-aware they were intellectually inferior to their offspring and it gave them little joy. However, what really struck a blow to their self-images was when their pre-teen daughters declared they could no longer reside in the same house with guardians who possessed so little appreciation for Ludwig Wittgenstein.

Thank God for Small Mercies

He managed to swerve away from the scurrying chipmunk, evade the oncoming Fed Ex truck, and avoid the group of school children on the sidewalk. *Lord*, he thought, *glad I missed that little critter.*

YOU NEVER KNOW WHAT TURNS-ON A RETIRED ACCOUNTANT

During a road trip out west, he'd spotted a piece of property for sale on the high plains of New Mexico, a few miles north of Corona on Route 54. It was a part of the country to which he was especially drawn. There was something about the wide-open spaces that grabbed him like no other place, and he'd often thought of retiring there. When he found out the two-bedroom house on the parcel came with 320 acres at a price he could well-afford, he jumped at it. Within weeks, he'd packed his home in Massachusetts, which he'd shared with his wife before her passing, and headed to the Land of Enchantment. Initially, loneliness had an impact on him but soon he felt at ease in his new surroundings. He would sip his morning coffee and gaze out at the endless horizon. Its effect was powerful, and he was often overcome with a sense of joy and well-being. Indeed, he felt closer to a higher power than he had at any time in his 68 years, and he wondered if things could possibly get any better. To his great satisfaction they did when one morning a group of Hell's Angels came riding up and declared he would now be sharing his dream house with them.

JUMPING TO CONCLUSIONS

When his friends found he was no longer alive, they couldn't believe it. "He wasn't that old. Still in his fifties and pretty fit," many of them said. "He seemed the picture of health. Always doing something outdoors. Watched what he ate," observed others. When they discovered he'd leapt from a seventh-story window, the nature of their comments changed.

Lofty Advice

Landing a plane was not something Everett expected he'd ever be doing, so to say he was ill-prepared to do so was an understatement. "No!" he blurted into the mouthpiece of his radio headset when the air traffic controller asked him if he knew how to operate the single-engine Cessna. "I'm just a passenger! What do I do? My uncle passed out. Not sure if he's even alive." Everett was advised to stay calm and to listen closely to the instructions he was about to receive. "Okay, okay," he gasped, watching in terror as the horizon tilted to one side and then the other. "This is important. Do you have something to write on . . . a pencil and paper?" He grabbed the small note pad and pen his uncle had used to record takeoff coordinates. "I do," he replied. "Good, now quickly write whatever you want to your loved ones and throw it out of the window so it won't burn up in the crash.

Repurposed

I was watching a YouTube video of Leonard Cohen this morning. He sure had it all. Warm personality, handsome as hell, great song writer, but what made me really jealous were those pipes of his. Holy shit! Think of the voiceover jobs I could have gotten with those.

DEEP DOWN EMOTIONS

He got an erection at the most inopportune times, like at a public swimming pool or when he was giving a class report. He wished he had better control of it, because when he needed to get an erection, he often couldn't get one, and that would upset his partner. "Is it because you don't find me attractive?" his girlfriend would ask. This made him feel bad, especially because feeling bad gave him an erection. Of course, when he felt bad, he didn't feel like having sex.

FLEXIBLE TRAVEL PLANS

They had scheduled a trip to visit their daughter and her family until she told them their house was surrounded by raging fires that had already taken the lives of most of their nearby neighbors. After their phone conversation, they decided it made more sense to go to the Caribbean after all.

What It Seemed Like to Him

Deep water fishing was a new experience for Felix. So, it was with mild trepidation he had accompanied his brother-in-law on a fishing excursion into the Cook Inlet for halibut. No sooner was his line baited and launched, his rod gave a powerful tug, nearly causing him to fall overboard. He pulled at the reel until his arm lost feeling and as his catch neared the side of the boat, a crewman hooked it aboard to a jarring cry. It landed near his feet and to his horror he saw he'd snagged a small gasping and flapping child. His impulse was to throw it back into the water, but he succumbed to the attaboys of his fellow anglers and had it filleted.

SOUR KRAUTS

A week following Hitler's triumphant arrival in London, the Fuhrer pronounced judgement on Winston Churchill. He would be executed one week hence before a public crowd in Parliament Square. Minister of Propaganda Joseph Goebbels indicated Hitler's decision as to the fate of Franklin Roosevelt would be announced following the Prime Minister's beheading.

Second Chance

I didn't understand Karl Ove Knausgaard's explanation for why he writes, or should I say I didn't appreciate his perspective on the subject, so I put his essay down and went on to something else. The next day, I began reading it again, and nothing had changed, so I put it down for the last time.

His Worst Day Ever

I felt the cold hand of fear grip me after my physical exam. "Let's talk in my office," said my doctor, in a solemn tone. "Get dressed and come right in." In less than a minute, I'd flung on my clothes and was tapping on his door. There was no answer. After a few more knocks, I inquired as to his whereabouts, and his receptionist said he'd gone out for some fresh air, adding. "But he told me to tell you to be sure to wait, because he has something important to tell you."

A SINFUL REPROACH

Henry was working on his piano variations, so I didn't want to interrupt him. I stood outside his studio until his playing stopped and then I tapped on the door. "Go away!" came his voice. "It's me, Jesus," I said and received a booming rejoinder. "I don't care if you brought Mary and Joseph with you . . . go away!" He often teased me about my name, but this time I'd had it. *Where'd I store the Caladium?* I wondered.

An Extraordinary Sight at Ocean Beach

A two-stack freighter emerged from behind the giant crags a few hundred yards off Cliff House as Jeb stood enjoying the sunset. *Big boat,* he thought and then he was surprised at just how large it actually was. As moments passed it continued to move south at high speed but without revealing its aft section. *My God, it must be two blocks long.* When it still hadn't fully overtaken the rocky outcroppings, he began to think it must be an illusion, although he was not one to see things that weren't there. *There's no ship that could possibly be that size though, so what's happening?* And then it lifted from the sea toward the heavens, a glowing water spout trailing it. *Okay, it has to be something the department of tourism came up with,* thought Jeb, following the levitating vessel with his squinting eyes as it vanished into the clouds.

Premature

We were in our farm's storm shelter as the tornado ripped away at the surface. We huddled against our pregnant mother's belly and listened to the voice of our future sibling as he/she (at that point we were unaware of the gender) told us we were going to die that very night. Three months later, after the early morning birth of our brother, we whispered in his ear that he should avoid making predictions.

THE JOYOUS EXPERIENCE OF NON-EXISTENCE

She wondered if being dead would be like it was before being born. If so, she was psyched. She couldn't recall a single moment during her lifetime as much fun as those prior to conception, which she also felt had been a genuine hoot.

Mary's Christmas

Lee's wife disappeared at Michael's Arts and Crafts. The plan was for him to wait in the car while she shopped for some holiday items. He'd listen to the football game on the radio and avoided dealing with the frenzied crowds—they made him jumpy and claustrophobic. After three-quarters-of-an-hour, he grew irritated, since she'd promised to be gone no more than 20 minutes. When another 15 minutes passed without her showing up, he was pissed and decided to go after her. By the time he was halfway down the first aisle his thoughts had shifted to how he'd retaliate for his wife's callous behavior toward him. *Fuck that bitch. I'll show her*, he thought. "Mary," he called, raising his voice only slightly, but soon he was shouting her name . . . but to no avail. *God help her when I get her. I'll* . . . After he'd searched every corner of the retail space, he sought out the manager, hoping to call for his wife over the intercom. "No, sir, I'm afraid that won't help," he was told. "Why? What do you mean?" questioned the irate spouse, fists clenched in assault mode. "Because she asked for our help and, in the spirit of the season, we offered it," answered the store supervisor, glancing at his watch. "And by now she's had enough time to get to the airport and make her flight before you can catch her."

COGNIZANCE

The sun rose harsh over the eastern most limits of Barstow, and Harris felt if he didn't hitch a ride by late morning, he'd be smart to return to town to seek shelter for the night. He didn't want to end up huddled against an alley dumpster as he'd done that night. Cops had actually cruised past where he lay without noticing him. He'd regarded that as a bit of good luck, certain he avoided arrest for vagrancy. How did he get to such a low point in his life, he wondered? Was it his drug addiction, recent felony charge, spousal abuse . . .? Why did he have to be taken down by things most guys got away with?

Recovered

He was laid low by what his doctors termed a thyroid storm. After several hours in ER, he spent three-weeks in ICU and then a week in post-critical care. The day he was moved to the general care ward, his wife informed him she would not be at their home when he returned . . . that she planned to divorce him. He was grateful the near-deadly storm had passed.

No Cupid in This Room

"I'd like to be able to write some romantic poems, but it just doesn't seem to be in my wheelhouse to think that way," lamented William.

"What way is that? You mean like the way stupid, dumb, mindless, dense, ignorant, shallow, witless, imbecilic, moronic, empty-headed humans do?" asked his friend.

"Yeah . . . *that* way," replied William.

Change of Plans

Raoul skipped down the stairs and abruptly stopped at the bottom. At both ends of the street were giant man-eating spiders preventing him from reaching the gym for his daily workout. *Bloody hell . . . this is getting old*, he thought, returning to his apartment.

A FLEXIBLE GUY

"You can't buy a quarter-acre of land and build even a shack on it for less than a million bucks around here," he was told by the first real estate office he entered in Bozeman, Montana. His hopes sunk along with the joy that had sustained him in the venture. For 20 years he'd saved everything he could to buy a little place in Big Sky country, and now it was apparent his few thousand dollars wasn't even down payment money. The only thing he could do was come up with a whole new plan . . . and that's exactly what he did.

Decision

He wondered if he would willingly die in place of his son. He thought it was asking a lot.

Getting the Party Started

He wondered if people were more sexually permissive than he was and, if so, was he missing out? Occasionally he sensed others were doing things he'd only fantasized doing. Did his wife screw around while she was away on business? Were the guys in his office making it with one another? Were there orgies going on in his neighborhood? He felt on the periphery of a good time and resolved to get out there and let his hair down.

Will Your Envy Kill the Love?

Look at you.

You soar.

You fly.

You reach the sky.

But me, you're brother,

where am I?

Echoed Sentiment

"'Lord love a duck,'" she'd say, reflecting on her troubled life. It was something she repeated often, and I wondered where she got the phrase. "It was a title from an old movie. Something that just stuck with me. Ducks don't have much luck when they're around people, and I haven't had much either, so *lord love a duck*." When I heard she'd been hit a by a car and died, all I could think was "Lord love a duck."

How the Road to Hell is Paved . . .

The dog next-door barked incessantly. Her owner was an elderly widow who would leave her outside for days at a time, regardless of the weather. I couldn't tell if she was being fed, except she was pretty skinny, and that bothered me nearly as much as her barking. So, I started feeding her, but it didn't work. In fact, she seemed to bark even more. *She's lonely*, I thought, so I let her into my yard and played with her. But when I went inside my house, she howled and wouldn't stop. *Okay, bring her in with you for a while*, I told myself and did. She was very happy with that, but when I tried to put her out, she refused to go, even growling at me. I called her owner to inform her of the situation, and she claimed she had no dog and hung up. Today, I'll take her to the vet to make sure she has her shots.

Fatal Attraction

Unlike his fellow oncologists, the aspect of his profession he most liked was informing patients they were dying. It wasn't that he was cruel or morbid, per se, it was just that he was first and foremost a student of human behavior in the context of hopelessness and despair. He had long made a study of how individuals reacted to devastating news and planned one day to publish his findings. "Oprah, here I come," he thought, preparing to meet with his next terminally ill patient.

The Last Resort

Snow was 10-feet high and piling. There was no walking from the cabin to safety. The wood supply was exhausted as was our food. The only candle left was about to flicker out. We would be in total frigid darkness in a matter of moments. It seemed there was no alternative but to use our teleporter to decamp to the Caribbean.

PEACE OF MIND

The builder urged her to invest in a safe room since the house was in a relatively secluded area and she spent so much time alone. After mulling over the idea, she agreed. The contractor assured her he would be the only other person aware of the hiding place, since he would be the only one doing the work. Not long after construction was completed, he went on a psychotic rampage and had not been seen since, although authorities believed he remained in the area.

AH-HA!

No matter how many different selfie poses he tried, he came out looking lined and haggard. There seemed no way to look younger than his 72 years. *So, this is what I actually look like,* he despaired, and then with relief he realized his phone was an older model.

DRESS REHEARSAL

Horrified by the prospect of death, Calvin thought if he staged his own funeral a few times he might lessen his fear. Thus, he purchased the least expensive casket he could find and set it up in a section of the basement in his small house. He hung black velour drapes on the walls surrounding the coffin and programmed his iPod to loop play Eric Clapton's "Tears in Heaven." For seven days straight, he climbed into the pine box, crossed his arms, shut his eyes and tried hard to imagine being dead. At the end of the week, his terror had morphed into a profound dread of being bored.

X Is My Way Forward

Wake up terrified

Dark outside window

Heart beats hard

Rise now or never

Creep through shadows

Is it coming?

Make it to bathroom

Too early for a pill?

No next without it

Swallow reprieve

An hour passes

Sky lightens

Inner demons darken

Another pill

Space between shortens

A palindrome

X is my way backwards, too

Coming and going . . .

Problems Come with Whatever You Think You Are

He didn't feel like a human. Neither man nor woman. Likewise, he had no sense of connection with any domestic or wild animals. But, maybe an arachnid, he thought. Yes, it was something closest to what he suspected he was. Of course, there existed the problem of how one would live as such.

Of Practical Necessity

The two recent Ivy League grads set out from Mandalgovi to Altai with planned layovers in Arvakheer, Bayankhongor, and Delger. Landing in Ulaanbaatar, Mongolia's largest city, they had bussed down to Mandalgovi, where they'd made arrangements for a vehicle to drive the 1,253 miles to Altai. It was an adventure the young friends had talked and dreamed about throughout their senior year and they had finally acquired the resources to make it happen. They'd prepped accordingly but had somehow overlooked the fact there was no Starbucks in the empty desert stretch they'd be traveling. When they discovered their mistake in Arvakheer, some 230 miles into their sojourn, the idea of immediately returning to Ulaanbaatar, where there was one Starbucks (albeit an imitation), struck them as quite reasonable.

PEST

A small bug climbed from under his collar and crossed his cheek. He did not acknowledge it, and I wanted to ask him why he didn't. Surely, he felt it, I thought. I withheld my question until another emerged from the same spot and took the identical path across his face. It was too much for me, and I expressed my disgust. "My God, young man, they're just trying to get to the forest," said he, pointing to his towering pompadour.

WEIGHING THE ADVANTAGE

I figure it's better to buy meat at a butcher, so I look through the Yellow Pages and locate a shop on the other side of town, about a half hour drive. I wonder if the meat, especially the calves-liver, will still be fresh by the time I get back.

There Are Times You Should See Your Doctor Unaccompanied

"Well, Mr. Jennings, you appear to have suffered a transient aphasia. It's a misfiring of your brain's electrical system. As you indicated, words you did not intend to say replaced those you did. Now, that in itself is nothing to worry about from a medical perspective, as it's a benign part of your silent migraines. Of course, you may have reason to be concerned about declaring your love for another woman in the presence of your wife.

Pursuing the Phantom

There was nothing that upset her more than waiting for a scheduled medical test, especially if it was for something she felt might determine her fate. While she counted off the days until her appointment, she Googled every potential outcome of her forthcoming procedure and always found they could lead to disaster. She'd fixate on the worst possible scenario until her nerves were ragged and her blood pressure at a dangerous level. When she finally got her results, no matter how favorable, she wasn't content until a test for a new symptom was scheduled.

When Someone Shows Love in a Special Way

The desktop on Kyle's computer had become a mystery. *How did the screenshot images of earwigs, lacewings, scorpionflies, barklice, strepsipterans, caddisflies, and mantids get there?* he wondered. The only thing he was certain of was someone clearly knew how to press his happy button.

Honeymoon in Morocco

Bay took a seat in the thread of shade on the terrace and removed the chechia he'd been given by an inebriated Aussie in the bar the night before. "You'd be smart to wear this on your walkabouts, mate," he'd advised. "Blending in is a wise thing for blokes like us in these parts." Now the red felt cap was damp from Bay's perspiration and strands of its tassel clung to his sunburnt neck. He knew it was foolish of him to wander the back streets of Casablanca, but he needed to get away from his new bride for a time. If not, he feared she would do something he would further regret. The boiling mint tea she'd flung at him earlier still caused him discomfort.

Things Would Probably Be Better If You Could Pick Your Birth Parents

My father owned a saxophone factory that made all kinds of saxophones—soprano, alto, tenor, baritone. I wasn't musical, and he held it against me.

This Is When Marge Would Benefit from Some Form of Distraction

Sometimes she thought she was already dead so why should she be afraid of something that already happened? Then she thought if she were aware her death had happened, she wasn't yet dead . . . and she became afraid again.

GALATIANS 6:7

The supermarket parking lot had only one place to dispense of empty shopping carts, and it was at the far end of the facility, so Marcus decided to roll it to where a bunch of others had been abandoned close by. As he approached it, an elderly woman was attempting unsuccessfully to park her vehicle. Next to the space to which she was aiming her heavily dented Corolla stood the cluster of carts. When Marcus put his there, the elderly driver yelled at him to move it so she could make a wider swing into the slot she was attempting to fill. Irked, Jamie asked if she wanted him to park her car, to which she replied, "Put the fucking cart where it belongs, dumb ass!" Shocked, he barked back, "Learn to drive, you old bag!" He then returned to his own car and drove away, feeling sheepish for having spouted off to her in the way he had. When someone in the car behind him at a stop sign shouted, "Move your goddamn car, old man!" he figured the Almighty was in payback mode.

144

PACIFICALLY

You would think with 200 eyes it would not fall prey to a simple deep fryer or skillet. But they are the utensils most responsible for decreasing the population of this creature, whose birth exceeds billions annually and decreases by nearly an equal number during the same period. Yet, despite this, there have been no reported incidents of this life form launching an offensive against its arch nemeses.

AMERICA RUNS ON . . .

According to Howard's *Fodors Travel Guide*, the resort city of Jurmala, Latvia, on the Gulf of Riga, offered many wonderful sightseeing opportunities, but without a Dunkin Donuts for his morning coffee and crumb cake muffin, he chose to remain on the tour bus hoping the four-hour stop-over would pass quickly.

A Curve in the Road

How stupid can you get setting out across the frozen Canadian tundra on your own to prove a hair-brained point? Craig chided himself. He'd told his drinking buddies at the Smokin Gun he could walk between Waskada, where he lived, and Melita, Manitoba, some 23 miles to the northwest, in six hours. Money was put on the bar and a wager was set. It was January and temperatures between the two provincial hamlets routinely dropped into the minus-zero category, even during daylight. He'd imposed dimwit challenges on himself before—some pretty nuts—but this one could kill him, especially since he'd be taking the so-called "as the crows fly" route far off the main road and any sign of civilization. "Every damn time you get sloshed you make dumb bets," he mumbled angrily. He'd been hiking two hours but wasn't really sure how far he'd traveled—hangovers did not enhance his cognitive abilities. *Probably a half-dozen miles. Shit, three times that to go,* he estimated. Already feeling exhausted, he stooped to catch his breath. It was then he caught site of a Burma Shave sign. "Huh, out here? What the hell!" When he couldn't find another one in any direction, he knew he was in deep trouble.

LATE AWARENESS

He hadn't really noticed how old he was beginning to look until recently. Indeed, his appearance had changed, and it wasn't for the better, as far as he was concerned. His hair had thinned and the lines around his eyes had grown more pronounced. Add to that, he felt his lips had shrunk and cheeks had hollowed. *A hell of a way to look at my 100th birthday party*, he moaned.

New Media

Sonya had great contempt for friends who took a long time to reply to her emails and texts. "What's the matter with people? Don't they get it? It's all about *quick* connection. That's what the technology's all about, for God's sake," she'd grumble when her inbox came up empty. After waiting an unusually long time to hear from one of her closest gal pals, she decided to resort to snail mail. A couple days later, and much to her surprise, she received a postal reply full of apologies and warm tidings. *Hmm, that's interesting,* she thought, inspired to send her other errant correspondents hardcopy posts as well. Again, the swift response time impressed her, but not as much as her novel form of communication impressed her friends.

INITIAL TEST

His PSA was on the rise, so his PCP suggested he get a Bx. Reluctantly, if not fearfully, he agreed and one was scheduled for the following TUES. There were no detectable NODS found during his DRE, and he took some solace in that. When he consulted with his URO DOC at MGH regarding the outcome of his biopsy, he was assured everything was OK and he had no CA. AWESO, he thought.

Tragic Assumption

She slipped him near beer trying to get him off his bender. The low (or no) alcohol beverage was told to help drunks get back on the wagon. She was desperate to get him sober again, because loaded he was violent. She wasn't aware that believing you're getting real booze was tantamount to getting real booze.

THERE ARE GHOSTS ENTERING YOUR HOUSE WHEN IT'S DARK

It had been one of the few nights Warren slept through without having to get up to pee, and he was thankful for that. He'd had too many sleepless nights lately. It was good to feel genuinely rested, and he was looking forward to a clear-headed, productive day at his writing desk. When he descended to the kitchen, he noticed a stream of cool air coming from the front room and checking its source was surprised and alarmed to find the main entrance door wide open. "What the hell . . .?" he mumbled, inspecting the surrounding yard and street. *I locked it, I know I did,* he told himself, closing the door and going to the kitchen. On his way, he picked up on another strong current and was nonplussed to find the back door ajar as well. *Okay, something is going on. This isn't kosher. Someone did this.* Warren then ventured to the basement bulkhead, and to his rising apprehension found it agape. He carefully secured all the entryways to the house and checked them multiple times throughout the day. His night was not restful obsessed as he was by the apparent encroachments into his home. To his relief, the next morning he found all of the doors securely shut but then noticed to his extreme dismay every window in the house was open.

TILL THE END OF TIME?

The day had finally arrived when humans had the chance to live forever through the miracle of a one-time pill. Most people took it, while a tiny handful decided they didn't want to stick around. Of the majority who opted for immortality, at least a third chose to abandon their present lives, claiming that being with the same family and friends for infinity was a form of purgatory.

STIMULUS

I'm told my brain scan is clear and for several minutes the joy of living returns. Everything feels better. I'm happy. But, I can't sustain it. Soon I'm back to my grey spot. The color gone. I need the brush dripping with death to reach the light.

This Time It Would Be Different

Until now Houston had been a bad luck city for Janice. Her two former trips there were embarrassing and painful. Failure to find the right job during her initial outing in the Texas metropolis had put her on its mean streets and a DUI fender bender on a visit three years later cost her probation and 12 hours in an alcohol education program. This time in H-Town she'd met a wonderful man whose former imprisonments were not going to keep her from marrying him and the happiness she knew she deserved.

GRATEFUL MOURNERS

Madeline charmed everyone at her wake, and that was her intent.
She'd been a terrible carper when alive and sought to make amends.

A LITTLE OFF THE FRONT

Across from our basement flat was Joe Oliver's Barber Shop. It was where I got my hair clipped when I was a small kid. Joe would do the cutting, and I liked him. He was real friendly and told me silly jokes while he chopped-away at my fast-growing locks. While I was in his chair, men would stream past and disappear behind a curtain that hung at the rear of the store. "Where they going?" I asked, to which Joe cryptically replied, "None of your beeswax, sonny." It left me forever curious about what was going on behind the floral shroud. When I brought up the subject with my parents, my father just smiled knowingly, while my mother said she no longer wanted me to have my hair cut there. "Something smells about that place," she declared. It was when several cop cars with their lights flashing showed up at Joe's that I figured the back room was where that smell came from.

The Curtains Part and the World Rushes In

The soft morning light seeps through the sheers and settles against his sleeping face. "Time to rise, honey," whispers his wife, who's been kneeling on the floor next to him and staring at him lovingly. "C'mon, my little cuddle bear. Rise and shine, darling," she continues, caressing his forehead. His eyes flutter like butterfly wings, and he gazes at her, mumbling, "I was dreaming I had diarrhea."

Fido's Fatal Flaw

He barked, and barked, and barked, and to her great frustration there was just no reasoning with the animal. "What can I do to get him to stop? she asked the vet. "Nothing short of putting him down," he answered. The dog owner considered it a reasonable solution.   ·

Too Much Information

For their first anniversary, Vera and Scott Freeman chose a visit to Quebec City and a stay at the fabled Chateau Frontenac. It was everything they hoped it would be, and the old town wrapped around the castle-like hotel reminded him of Europe, although he'd never been to the continent. "This must be just like Paris," he'd commented to his wife, who replied that it did remind her of the time she'd been there. Scott did not pursue the observation any further, since he knew she'd been overseas with her former boyfriend, and he did not like thinking of his new wife with another man. That, however, didn't keep Vera from adding that the City of Light was the most romantic place in the world. It prompted a counter-offensive from her husband, one he would immediately regret. "Well, Quebec City has to be the best place for *sex* in the world . . . huh, honey?" Her silence cast a dark cloud over the remainder of his holiday.

Special Delivery

Helga waited anxiously to receive her husband's severed head. He'd been decapitated for refusing to pledge loyalty to the Nazi Party as a conscientious objector. It had been a long drawn out affair, with endless useless appeals in Salzburg and Berlin. When part of him reached home she hoped she might gain some sense of closure to the worst experience of her young life. She prayed the Reichpost would not lose the package as they had so many times before.

A Dog's Life

Every time the Jamesons fought, their rescue dog would slink away and hide for fear she was the cause of the discord. This ultimately resulted in her running away and being seized by the town's animal warden. She had no identification and was earmarked for extinction. Just as she was about to be euthanized, she was taken to a northern city, where she was adopted by a loving couple . . . who soon fell out of love.

His Friend's Response to His Complaints[1]

"One thing at a time. Our goal is to be the fittest, most cantankerous old bastards we can be. Simple as that. Work on snarls and guffaws each day, more important than pushups. It's what separates us from the riff raff of humanity. We are unique . . . special riff raff. Of the wrinkled and balding variety. So, revel in it."

---

[1] Special thanks to Larry Collette on the occasion of our continuing deterioration.

Apptitude

The company had made a terrible mistake, one that would prove fatal. It had failed to create a built-in obsolescence app for its product. Now it would be just a matter of time before its customers would no longer need its new models.

An Inside Theory

Leo would be double scoped (endoscopy/colonoscopy) at the hospital to determine what was causing his stomach issues. For months he experienced intense gas, diarrhea, nausea, abdominal aches, vomiting, and significant weight loss. As the day of the procedure approached, the symptoms seemed to abate, causing him to question whether he should cancel the appointment. "No, you should go through with it. It may come back full bore, and it may even be worse? Let's find out what's going on once and for all," advised his wife. He agreed with her, and the day to be probed arrived. After the scopings his doctor informed him it wasn't an intestinal issue at all. With a mix of relief and frustration, he asked what it was if not a lower GI problem. "We're baffled," admitted the gastroenterologist. "Nothing out of the ordinary showed up, so we can only conclude that your intestinal track has been invaded by a malevolent force capable of invisibility when scrutinized by human examiners." It wasn't what Leo wanted to hear, but at least it was something to go on, he figured.

EVERYTHING OLD IS NEW AGAIN[ii]

He knew sooner-than-later the Internet would fail, and he'd be back to regular old books. *Shit . . . what's my password?* he wondered.

[ii] Title appropriated from Peter Allen and Carole Bayer Sager.

Delirium Dames

In the two-dollar a night hotel in Harbinger, South Dakota, he fought a deep fever and racking cough. Though it was late Spring, a frosty wind pierced the thin walls of his tiny room. There he drifted in and out of consciousness at once aware of his grave situation and beguiled by the showgirls who danced across the room's ceiling in their sequined leotards.

A Moving Experience

For 30-years, Walt had driven a semi on the backroads of the west, hauling petroleum equipment to remote sites. It was something that gave him pleasure, because he loved rolling through the majestic hinterlands of the region. In all, it was a satisfying way to make a paycheck, and he'd managed to bank quite a bundle. When he took early retirement, he decided to buy a place in the area he'd been traveling for so many years. *Be nice just to settle in the foothills of the Salt River Range or Big Horn Mountains,* he thought, and he did just that. One-hundred-forty-eight acres and a two-bedroom cabin were his for a price he could well afford. However, it wasn't long after he moved in he became restless and went back to work, concluding things just didn't look quite as good when they stood still.

JOHN COUGAR SNEAKING PUFFS WITH JOHNNY CARSON

They're both smokers and between commercial breaks they satisfy their habit. When the stage manager shouts "Back in five, four . . ." they douse their butts and purge their lungs, clearing the smoke with their waving hands. "So, John, you're going to sing your latest hit," says Johnny, holding up an empty album jacket.

Slow to Convince

Jerry thought it was ridiculous that Mel was naming his bar The Skidmark. He didn't see the humor in it and thought it was foolish for him to name his new business with a term possessing such a crude connotation. When Mel installed a neon-sign featuring a pair of boxer shorts with a flashing brown streak up their middle, Jerry thought he'd carried the whole thing too far. "That's nothing, check this out," Mel chortled, opening the entrance door to the saloon. Jerry had to admit the loud farting noise that followed brought it all together.

THE FLOWERS OF 1955

They're definitely different than they are in the 2020s. Deeper color and greater fragrance. Larger, too . . . more robust. What's happened to nature in the intervening decades? It has to be human pollution that changed things, he thinks. He's almost too ashamed to take the time travel machine back to the present age. But his time away from Gurugram has expired.

THE UNENDING JOY OF LONGEVITY

He'd lived so long, he'd lost his ability to taste food.

"It's not unusual for someone 161 years-old to lose his palate. It's one of the many characteristics of Methuselah Syndrome," observed the geriatrician.

"Oh, great. What's next? My dick falling off?"

"Good, I see you've been Googling."

A Long and Charmed Life

Suddenly the Cessna single engine plane took a nose dive and try as he might, the pilot was unable to pull out of it. It ended up crashing into a farmhouse and killing those on board as well as four people on the ground. As firemen and police sorted through the debris they discovered a fully intact birthday cake with the lettering "Happy 100th." Later in the day, the passenger to whom the cake was intended returned to the scene on an electric unicycle.

FATE CAN BE A BASTARD

It was on the loneliest stretch of the high-plains in eastern Montana that Larry's car broke down. There he sat in his 12-year-old Chevy Silverado looking out of its windows and rearview mirrors hoping to see a car that might come to his aid. But hours came and went and he began to worry that he might have to spend the night where he was. He knew from the map that there was no town for dozens of miles, so walking was out of the question. Now as the sun began to set, he worried that the temperature might go below zero, even though it was late April. *I'll freeze to death out here unless someone comes along and stops,* he told himself. As things turned out, that's exactly what happened . . . no one came along.

HE WAS NOT KNOWN FOR HIS PRACTICALITY

Route E40 was the longest road in Europe, some 8,000 kilometers, and it was Kenneth's plan to drive it end to end. He only lacked a vehicle and the monetary resources to underwrite the venture. *So, what?* he thought, not to be thwarted by small details.

KILLJOY

To pass the time we watch old YouTube videos of late 19th and early 20th century street scenes until my husband says, "You know, all those people are long since dead." After his comment, I feel like I'm watching zombie movies and I'm creeped out. I tell him so, and he replies, "You listen to all those old radio comedies, and you can bet everyone you hear laughing is dead, too, not to mention the performers." I decide I should find something to pass the time without him.

LOCAL REMEDY

It was comforting to Frank to live within a short drive of the greatest hospital in America. This time he was certain he had something really serious.

Tick-Tock

We constantly talk about how time is running out for us and what we should do about it. "Better act now, because in five or six years we're not going to be as physically able to get around. Damn, we'll be 80," says my brother-in-law. It's part of our daily harangue against the northern climes and the need to move to Florida with our wives. I agree, "Yeah, if we wait much longer, it won't be worth it. We'll be too frigging old to enjoy the sunny life there." It's mostly the winters that have us in this anxious state of mind. When the weather turns warmer, we forget that the black ice with our expiration dates imbedded in it is just around the corner.

Respectful Rival

In 1965, author and civil rights activist James Baldwin scored a decisive victory over Conservative spokesman William F. Buckley during their debate at Cambridge University. It was not with graciousness that Buckley shook hands with what he'd frequently referred to as "that queer little negro."

Road Sign

He needed to paste something to his car's dashboard to remind him not to go so crazy that he'd do something dumb, resulting in tragedy. So, he came up with the letters TAM that stood for Traffic Anger Management. It was his hope they'd signal him the dangers of his impatience in highway snarls and keep him from an awful act. They had worked for a while and then became amorphous, like so many symbols or mantras. That was a shame for those who survived . . . and those who didn't.

Hot Springs

He's an elderly widower, but he still gets an erection. This mostly happens when he thinks of the sex he had with his deceased wife, but occasionally it occurs when he looks at the naked women in his old Playboys, in particular the photo of Stella Stevens. He thinks of her as the Youth of His Fountain.

Blood Wedding

Famed Spanish poet Federico Garcia Lorca was obsessed with death. It was his true lover. He courted it tenaciously in his poems and plays. It was not an unrequited love long.

Rewrite

He couldn't say one of his lines in the play without breaking up in the middle of it. No matter how he tried, he would reach a point in the passage and start cackling like a hyena. This was not good given that it was a very serious drama and the line itself was pivotal to the scene. Furthermore, it was not intended to be humorous. But how could he possibly say "It was the baloney sandwich that caused him to choke to death" without losing it? None of the other actors thought the sentence particularly funny, but for reasons he could not explain, it triggered hysterics in him. Finally, the director suggested they change the line to read, "It was the salami sandwich that caused him to choke to death." It immediately resolved the issue.

Omen

She worked hard to be accepted into the space program. She wanted nothing more than to be an astronaut. When she was invited to join NASA, she was ecstatic. Her mood changed when her Dodge Challenger caught fire on the way to Houston.

MICKEY FINN TIME MACHINE

It's downtown Ventura, California, in 1930, and he doesn't know how he got there. He remembers drinking something someone gave him and thinking it tasted better than anything he ever had . . . heaven in a glass. *But, Jesus Christ,* he reflects, *nothing tastes good enough to lose 90 years over.*

Things Generally Work Out

For 22 two days in a row, Calvin has attempted unsuccessfully to stay cool in the midst of a record-breaking heatwave. He has tried everything but resists the idea of installing central air conditioning in his house. *It will cost a fortune, and I just can't afford it*, he thinks. But he's miserable in his steamy raised ranch. Then his nephew suggests he place a window AC in the room where he spends most of his time. He likes the idea and goes to Lowes but because of the hot spell, they are out of window units. It is refreshingly cool in the giant box store, so he decides he'll hideaway in it at closing time and spend the nights there until the scorcher breaks. After three evenings enjoying the cool comfort of the store, he returns home because the temperature has dropped significantly and his house is habitable again. He now has a plan for future heat waves that will save him a bundle of money, and he is pleased. *If the boiler breaks, I have a place to go in the winter, too*, he tells himself, happier still.

GIVING UP THE GHOST

Nothing would help Craig get to sleep. He tried everything, including over the counter remedies, prescription drugs, rest exercises, and insomnia therapy. Finally, he decided to stop fighting it, figuring he'd just stay awake. *Fuck sleep*, he told himself, and that worked until Sponge Bob Square Pants tried to kill him.

Adventures in Tourism

The two young women were going to a country fair in Tata, at least that's what they thought. They had either misunderstood or were misinformed by the travel guide in Tangier because the festival in that remote Moroccan village was dedicated to the celebration of desert amblypygids of the *Musicodamon atlanteus* variety. As soon as they arrived and saw hundreds of six-legged creatures crawling all over the narrow town square, they decided to return immediately to their Disney Cruise ship.

LIFE DOES NOT ALWAYS IMITATE ART

He wrote a stunningly beautiful book of love haikus, which countered everything people thought they knew about him. All he seemed interested in up to that point was field-dressing the animals he killed during hunting season.

*IN THE MIDDLE GROUND BETWEEN LIGHT AND
SHADOW . . .*

It wasn't until a few minutes later as Cal was driving down the road that he thought about the directions he'd been given by the convenience store clerk. In haste, he hadn't questioned them, just nodded thanks and shot away. Now he realized they were nonsensical. "What the hell is 'take the second right on your left?'" he mumbled to himself, making a U-turn back to the store to confront the attendant about the screwy directions he'd been given. "Oh, sorry," said the smirking youth, "I meant take the second *left* on your *right*." *Now that makes more sense,* thought Cal.

SPAM STEW

He wanted to make a lamb stew on Day 89 of the Coronavirus shelter-in-place order but due to the meat shortage, his local market was out of what he needed. He thought about what else he could use and discovered there were options. This realization kept him from losing it entirely.

Confidence

He worked very hard at his art, spending long hours daily refining his novel. He'd heard somewhere it took the average writer a minimum of two-to-four years to finish a book, and he'd been laboring on his for over a decade. Given his significant investment of time, he was certain he'd created a bestselling masterpiece. He was *not* an *average* writer.

Fleeting Recognition

Perry was informed he was to receive an award for his book of prose/poetry. It was the first such recognition in his writing career, and although he hadn't heard of the literary prize, he was thrilled to get the call. Some of his excitement left him when he was told a ten-dollar coupon to Wendy's would accompany the laurel.

Three Songs Lennon Never Got to Write

"Randoff the Dark-Eyed Junco"

"Take Her All My Yestermorns"

"Happy Merry Sarah Barrow"

First Things First

Motion detectors were installed on all four corners of his house designed to provide a 360-degree illuminated view of his property at night should there be an intruder. It was a significant investment, so when he saw the silhouette of a giant object wielding a long knife move past his kitchen window without activating the security lights, he immediately called his electrician to complain.

In Plain Sight

Let's see where this goes, he thought, facing the blank page. His goal was to write 250 words before noon each day until he had a story. The first challenge he faced was the lack of an idea. A plot line was simply not forthcoming, but when the clock struck 12, he felt he'd accomplished something just by thinking about it. The next day brought the same creative vacuum, and for two weeks he found nothing to write about. Frustrated with his lack of productivity, he blamed his writer's block on the distraction caused by the recent activity outside his office window, at which he decried, "How can anyone come up with an idea with you damn woolly mammoths stomping around out there?"

WEAK GENES

For the heck of it, Sharon Googled the names of her long-dead parents and found no entries for them. She was not surprised. *What had they done of any notice?* she thought. She then went to images, and after scrolling past countless unfamiliar faces, there they were. Initially, she only vaguely recognized them but upon closer inspection realized they were photos from an old family album her brother had. They were in their twenties, she calculated, and were not what anyone would consider attractive people. Suddenly her ancient resentment resurfaced. They had passed on so little to her in the looks department . . . so very little.

Firewalling It

He had his plans for the day. They consisted of a stop at the grocery store, bank, and gas station. He was thankful he had things to do. The approaching killer asteroid had consumed his thoughts lately and begun impacting his mood. Tomorrow he would go to the dry cleaners and pharmacy. It was important to keep busy to prevent plunging into a state of hopelessness and despair.

SILENCE OF THE LAMB

No Shepherd's pie I've ever tasted was as wonderful as my sister, Wanda's. Then I order one at an inn in a remote village in northern England and that changes. It is not merely better than Wanda's, it is quite literally beyond words. I ask the chef if I might have the recipe, and he chuckles. "Oh, but sir, it is as much from the cask as it is from the cupboard," he replies cryptically and disappears, only to return a couple minutes later holding a can labeled Dorset Cottage Pie. When I email Wanda about my discovery, I don't hear from her. Nor is she at the airport to pick me up as planned when I return home.

CULTURAL CONTRASTS

Singh ate his white ant egg soup with gusto, excitedly anticipating the fried beetle and silkworm stew to follow. It was such a relief to have returned to Laos after months in America eating ambrosia fruit salad.

When It's Time to Reevaluate a Career Choice

Winston doubled down on Xanax before entering the classroom. It calmed him and kept him from going over the edge. Teaching first graders depleted his reserves. No matter how hard he tried to explain the work of Immanuel Kant, they just didn't seem to get the philosopher.

He Wasn't Good with Names

Crossing the North Sea was always a bit risky late Spring, but he'd sailed it from Lowestoft, England, to Leiden, Netherlands, twice before and felt confident about the crossing this time. It turned out to be a grievous mistake on his part. Halfway between the land masses, his 18-foot skiff began taking on water due to a severe squall. Sensing with good reason he and his wife were not going to make it, he suggested they pray, although he'd forgotten who the patron saint of sailors was. It was just after their boat sunk, taking them with it, that a cargo ship passed over their watery grave. A crew member on its deck swore he heard a female voice screaming a series of expletives at someone called Brendan.

The Lasting Impact of Early Experiences

He kept flashing back to the worst days of his childhood—there'd been two. The image of his beloved dog being struck by a truck had been seared into his memory and it brought him to tears each time it reasserted itself. The other worst day of his childhood was even more upsetting for him and had to do with discovering Darth Vader was the bad guy. The memory of it, like that of his dead dog, would continue to haunt him.

Some Things More Precious

The undulating rainbow-colored screen-saver image reflects in the unclosed eyes of the corpse. It is that more than anything that spooks the murderer, who's returned to the scene of the crime to retrieve his copy of *Don Ho's Greatest Hits*.

REMAINS OF THE DAY

After 38 years of marriage their sex life was at its lowest ebb. The couple remained dedicated to one another but the erotic aspect of their relationship had faded like the scent of a week-old corsage. He found his stimulation fly fishing and his wife stitching Amish quilts. To maintain the illusion of a conjugal relationship, they would engage in occasional pedestrian sex, usually doggy-style over the arm of the living room recliner. During one of their customary Friday night restaurant outings, he raised the idea of watching porn together as a means for restoring some zest to their sex life, but his spouse showed little interest. "Well, is there something else that might turn you on?" he asked. They sat in silence for several moments, and then she hailed their server for the dessert menu.

Was It Because He Hated Mrs. Hodge's Class?

My fifth-grade friend, Jeffrey, used to punch himself in the nose to cause himself to bleed so he could be sent to the nurse's office.

WHERE IS JIM PATE?

Big brother-type to me. Six years older. College graduate. Always interested in stuff I said. "With that imagination, you'll go places, Mike." I knew he would, too . . . maybe a president of something. Definitely a big deal in the future. Planned on law school when he served his time. Drafted from a small town in Tennessee. Drove a VW bug. Told him I was getting a Cadillac someday. He smiled whenever I said that. "Why not two?" he'd joke. Never saw him after I was discharged. Googled him 45 years later. No luck finding him. Drive a low-mileage Ford Fusion. Like new.

How Technology Cheats Us

It occurs to her she can actually hear and see the author she's currently reading and she sets his novel aside and goes to YouTube. After watching him discuss his work for hours, she feels little urge to return to his book.

THE PURSUIT OF . . .

She was the perfect body-type to Bram, and he so desperately needed that body-type, but he'd had no success attracting anyone whose physique came close to it, and it was driving him to think bad thoughts. On one of his early morning walks he saw a woman who epitomized his sexual fantasies and trailed after her. He had reached the point it was time to satisfy his punishing hunger . . . whatever the cost. He kept a safe distance so as not to arouse her suspicion as she jogged up Boylston Street to Massachusetts Avenue and then reversed her direction down Newbury Street to the Boston Gardens, where she shifted direction again running the length of Beacon Street to Kenmore Square. Completely spent, Bram watched in frustration as his prey disappeared west on Commonwealth Avenue. Unable to continue his pursuit, he staggered into Sal's Pizzeria for a piece of consolation.

Literally Disliked

Gustave Flaubert hated George Sand

Harold Bloom hated J.K. Rowling

Vladimir Nabokov hated Fyodor Dostoevsky

Virginia Woolf hated Aldous Huxley

Mark Twain hated Jane Austen

Truman Capote hated Jack Kerouac

Elizabeth Bishop hated J.D. Salinger

D.H. Lawrence hated James Joyce

Ernest Hemingway hated William Faulkner

Dylan Thomas hated Rudyard Kipling

Gertrude Stein hated Ezra Pound

Evelyn Waugh hated Marcel Proust

Henry James hated Edgar Allen Poe

. . .

Last Sentiment

His eyes followed her body as it fell from the 420-foot cliff to the rocks below. He'd tripped on something near the edge of the peak and grabbed at his wife's arm to right himself. It had caused her to plunge from the precipice. He was certain he'd seen her lips form the words "clumsy asshole" as she descended to her death. His spouse's heartfelt utterance would be kept close to his heart for the remainder of his days.

His Body Has Not Yet Been Found

I lay here dead. The blood of my mortal wound sipped by flies. Thank God, I don't feel the cold of the desert night. Mother was right, there's always something to be grateful for.

A Little Encouragement

After several years writing short stories, he concluded there was nothing of genuine literary merit among them. He'd assembled what he felt were his best works to send to a press, but given his negative assessment, he scrubbed the idea. *It would never be published, so you might as well find something else to do with your life. Writing is just not for you,* he told himself, his spirits at a new low. He suddenly changed his mind when his friend told him he loved the story about human waste devouring Martians. "It was really good, especially the part when they all get terrible gas and set their spaceship on fire." It was enough to get the would-be author back to his keyboard.

GHOST TRAIN

There never was better fun to Clarence than riding the rails from Fayette to Bibb. The off-road countryside in Alabama had held endless fascination for him his entire life, and he was determined to have a go at the freight run one last time before his 90th. He kept the specifics to himself, knowing his kids would object to it on the grounds of his lame right leg. "Paw, we don't care none 'bout you bein' old, cuz you got your vitals. Just that twisted limb a yours gonna' cause you trouble doin' anything major physical," they'd said when he mentioned in passing he'd like to jump the Autauga for old time's sake. So, it was hush about his doing so now. A day before his birthday celebration, he slipped from the house and drove his old pickup to where he recalled hopping the coal cars a half century earlier. To his surprise and disappointment, he couldn't locate any tracks, and when he managed to talk with someone, he was told there'd never been a train in that region of the state. Clarence just smiled and winked at the stranger. He knew better.

Desperate Times Call for Desperate Measures

It wasn't enough he never felt good but now he was cold all the time. No matter how many blankets he piled on his bed, it remained frigid. The fabrics never warmed when he was against them, because his flesh and bones had ceased to give off heat. He was alive but his body had stopped behaving as if it were. *Oh, well,* he thought, *maybe bungee jumping will get my blood flowing.*

A Perfect Score

Since he'd never even held a rifle, it struck him as sheer folly he'd qualified as an Expert marksman on the gun range in basic training. It resulted in his being assigned to the United States Army Sniper School at Fort Benning. There he repeated his serendipitous performance and was sent to Afghanistan. When he returned from his deployment and was discharged from the service, he was constantly asked by friends how many people he had killed. He would say nothing, wishing to keep to himself the fact that he'd successfully shot no one.

CERTITUDE

He knows he has a terminal disease, but his doctor claims he's in good health. Who's the better judge of how he feels than himself? he thinks, and he doesn't feel well at all. He has a great pain in the vicinity of his liver, and despite all the tests indicating his liver is fine, he knows it's not. So, he'll hold to his belief it's the source of what is killing him. He's heard many people say doctors don't know everything.

LIFE FULFILLED

What really upset him about dying was leaving the open road and his beloved camper van. He'd made a wonderful life for himself the last few years, and he was thankful for the joy he'd experienced traveling and meeting new people. Now, as he faced his final sunset, he thanked his maker for allowing him to reach Wakeeney.

An Act of Compassion

She was about to turn 47 and had never been married. In fact, had never been in a so-called serious relationship. Had only had sex with one person and then only one time. She was not unattractive. In fact, by contemporary standards, she was quite lovely. Why she remained without a partner troubled her parents, and it didn't matter to them what gender her soulmate might be. Another woman would be fine, as long as their daughter was with somebody. They felt her loneliness very deeply, and it detracted from what small joy existed in their own lives. Finally, it all became too much for them to bear, and they decided to take action. They purchased her a singles cruise and while she was away they moved and left no forwarding address.

Is It Asking Too Much?

I'm a leaf in the world's largest forest, a grain of sand on an unnamed beach. Would you look for me if the fate of humanity depended on it?

"CAN YOU SPARE A FARTHING, MY LORD?"

London's homeless women frequently installed themselves on the benches in Spitalfields Gardens in the early 1900's. It was the practice of the friendless poor to plead for a handout from passersby. Occasionally, their outstretched palms would be met with the saliva of passersby. It was not how the park came by its name.

Omnipresence

The log cabin nestled against the foothill of a towering peak in the snowcapped Fairmont Range stood as a beacon of salvation to Ray Billington. It was only after he'd climbed a treacherous rocky slope to scout out anything that might lead to civilization that he'd spotted it. It was the answer to his prayers, since he was convinced he may never reach safety. It had been three days since he'd been separated from the Holy Spirit Hikers Club and he was out of food and water. *Thank you, God. I knew you'd be there for me,* he muttered, scrambling in the direction of the shelter. As he approached it, he let out an anguished cry, "Are you fucking kidding me? A Christian Science Reading Room?"

SIMILAR BUT DIFFERENT

Ernest Hemingway and Hart Crane were born on the same day in the same year. They also had suicide in common, although they did not die on the same day . . . nor did they use the same method to end their lives.

Concession

There were people in the garage, at least two. Franz wasn't sure how long they'd been there. Last week he'd noticed them for the first time. They looked like shadows . . . silhouettes. It was difficult to discern any physical characteristics, but he was certain they were humans, unlike the aliens he'd seen the month before. They moved about every time he went to deposit something in the trash barrels. The first time he saw them, he called them out, but they didn't respond, just kept shuffling between the ride-on mower, compressor, and snow blower at the far end of what was more a storage area than a space for cars. When Franz mentioned them to his wife, she went out to look for herself but found no one. He then accompanied her to the garage, and they were there to him but not to her. "Okay," she said, following a long sigh, "Let's just call them your *new* little friends."

Upper Hand

A young Nazi soldier was pleasuring himself in the Black Forest, when an American G.I. came upon him.

Sibling Rivalry

It's a well-known fact beloved crooner Bing Crosby was a terrible father to his first four sons. In an early photo of his initial family one can sense his sons are unhappy. In a photo featuring his second family and fifth son, one can understand why the early Crosby boys would like to beat the shit out of their much younger half-sibling.

Conversion

He's bewildered by his friend's former statement that being Catholic defined who she was when she switches to Judaism after meeting her new husband.

Off Their Asses

They rode mules to the canyon's floor. It had been a frightening descent to them but well worth it. The views were spectacular. Now, as they were about to return to the top, neither could muster the courage to make the trek back. The trail leader assured them it was safer to go up on the animals than down, but they resisted the idea, asking to be taken out of the canyon along the river's edge. "It flows to flat land, doesn't it?" they inquired. "Eventually, yes, but it's a very long way and then there's just more desolation. Besides, we don't have the time or supplies with us to do it. There are other people to consider, too" he replied, with growing frustration. Unable to convince the couple to return with the group, he decided he'd come back for them once he'd led the remaining party back to basecamp. "Stay where you are, and I'll ride you out, okay?" When he arrived on the scene hours later, the couple were nowhere to be found. They'd decided to take matters into their own hands and exit the canyon without him. After two days on foot, the pair were nearly exhausted. They had not been able to get the mules to budge from where they were. Soon they'd run out of water and granola bars and consequently could hardly summons the energy to move another step forward. Then they spotted what appeared to them a Capitol Grille at the end of the gorge. "Well, there you are," they muttered, broadly smiling to one another

A Decline in the Dependability of Universal Air Travel

The earlier than scheduled arrival on Earth was an inconvenience for those in premium class about to partake of the most recently captured prey in GN-z11. "Three hundred-point-seven million light years to destination, my prehensile tale!" squawked a passenger.

Mama Said It Was His Special Place, but We Never Knew Why

At least twice a year, Daddy would take my baby sister and me on a Sunday ride to Tryon. It was an hour drive from our house in North Platte, and along the way we'd stop for a picnic lunch in a field with a big Cottonwood tree. As soon as we got to Tryon, Daddy would turn the car around and we'd head home. We didn't mind going there so many times, but when we got a little older we asked why he always took us to the same place. "'Cause . . ." he answered.

How Great Things Are Born

Lavlos Slaminski wondered if his existence meant anything at all. With eight billion members of his species on the planet, how could it? he reasoned. *I'll have to do something really special to stand out.*

THE GODS IN OBJECTS

The humidor held 12 cigars and he knew it should never contain less than eight. The voice had told him. Only this once had he let it get down that low, and he rushed to the smoke shop to restock it. To his chagrin, he'd found the tobacconist closed, and he feared returning to his apartment for the rebuke that awaited.

It Was Their Secret

Each night around ten he took his dog out to relieve herself in the field next to his house. He was always a little apprehensive about what he might find. In the past, he'd encountered deer, raccoons, fox, skunks, and coyotes. Tonight, the motion light set to flood the quarter acre lot revealed something quite extraordinary. Not 20 feet before him stood his deceased best friend. For several moments, he was frozen in place, but when the perfectly preserved corpse greeted him in the voice he'd known most of his life, his fear melted away. Until his own death two years later, he would meet up nightly with his old chum and talk about anything that interested them—vintage cars, sports, and shapely women were the dominant topics. He told no one about the nocturnal visits to insure they would continue when they took up residence in another friend's backyard.

A Lousy Time to Confront Your Limits

She calculated the gap between the roofs to be at least 20 feet. She'd won ribbons at school in the broad jump, but her record was far short of what she needed to escape the Rottweiler that had chased her to the top of the building.

Under Observation

For several nights, Arthur dreamt he was wandering in a desert only to end up on a street in a rundown section of a strange city. He tried to figure out what the dream meant, but failed to decipher it. At his therapy session, he was told the experience held special significance for him. When he asked what it was, he was advised to try to interpret it himself before the next meeting. "I'd like to hear from you before positing my professional opinion." Over the next week he tried to demystify the phantasm but came up empty. When his therapist asked if he'd discovered the dream's meaning, he admitted he hadn't. After a long thoughtful pause, she replied, "Well, it probably wasn't that important anyway, so I wouldn't lose any sleep over it."

Responsibility

He had a routine of filling his dog's water dish whenever he left the house. He worried that if something should happen to him, it could die of thirst, and he did not want that on his conscience, even if he were dead himself.

Little Maurice Was Not a Nice Child

He caught bugs with fly paper and severed their legs, causing their bodies to drop into the bowl of gruel he carefully placed in the path of their descent. Breakfast was his favorite meal.

Cueing Up

He didn't want to be the first to go. Yet he knew the loss of a loved one would be hard to take. Still, he didn't want to die before anyone else. He would take a spot in line behind any of his relatives or friends, with the exception of his wife. Even then, he wondered whether he'd let her slip in behind him.

TRANSCENDENT LOVE

He was killed in 1915 by a bomb dropped from a deathly quiet German dirigible. He'd taken his bicycle to his sweetheart's house and was only a couple kilometers from it when his end came. He was the first love of her life, and they'd just pledged lifelong fidelity to one another. "Does a vow you make to someone when they're alive count when they're dead?" she'd asked her parson a month after the tragedy. "If they're no longer effected by it, I would think not," he'd answered, whereupon she felt a profound need to praise her lord.

YOU JUST DON'T KNOW

He figured he'd go just like Glen Ford did in Superman. Be walking back to the house and drop. He was wrong though. He was trimming the hedges when his ticker gave out.

"Crazy Little White Men Live in Box!"

Eighty-one-year-old Tashunka lived in what amounted to little more than a lean-to 14-miles north of Wanblee in the northeast section of the Pine Ridge Reservation. He had resided in the dilapidated dwelling alone since his pregnant wife and children moved away from the inadequate space to a relative's larger house. Tashunka remained behind to tend to their livestock. Every couple of weeks his youngest daughter would bring him needed staples and help with any chores he was unable to perform. "Why don't you come live with us, Ate? It would be easier for you," Kimimela would ask, but the elder would not hear of it. "Chetan, the eagle spirit, lives here. I live here. This is the place of my spirit, too. Why would I leave?" During one of her routine visits, she brought a small transistor radio to give to her father. "It will keep you company," she told him. In all his years, he had never seen such a device. When she turned it on, loud rock music flowed from it, prompting Tashunka to strike it with his walking stick and bellow words in a tongue she hardly knew.

DEAD ANIMAL HOUSE

Cats kept turning up deceased in Jacob's backyard, and it wasn't due to foul play. It was because they were very old, reported the veterinary clinic where he took a half dozen of the dead felines. "Why are they dying in my yard," he inquired? To which the vet answered, "It could be because your house is perched atop an ancient burial ground for animals and they're drawn to it in their last moments of life. You ever see 'Poltergeist'?" Jacob thought about that possibility and decided it wasn't likely. *Just cats*, a*nyway*, he thought. However, the following week he discovered several dead coyotes on his property. As had been the case with the cats they, too, were declared to be quite elderly and free of signs of foul play by the vet, who again posited the idea of an ancient animal cemetery. It was moments after Jacob discovered a dead rhino next to his patio that he called a realtor.

Keen Thinking at an Early Age

He'd heard that covering an animal's eyes would keep them from going wild, so he figured that's what he'd do to his mom when she discovered he'd broken the finial on her cherished Tiffany lamp.

Life Decisions

His wife was gone. In what was viewed by authorities as a freak accident, his partner of 37 years was no longer the major presence in his life she had been. Now he had to make a decision. Remain in their home of over two decades or move? A tough decision. He liked the old colonial he and his spouse had rescued from near dilapidation, but he'd long dreamed of a change . . . maybe owning a piece of land out west. Nothing grand, although now he could afford it. Just a place right for him and his beloved ten-year-old Boxer, Ally. Perhaps a horse to trail around the open range, if there was enough open range around the few acres he'd own. So, it was decision time—go or stay. His only child lived in France and had for five years, and apart from a friend or two, there was little to hold him in suburban Boston. *So, go*, he thought, and the idea excited him. First, he'd head out to New Mexico and shop around for a nice piece of real estate. The Taos area had always attracted him, so he'd travel there right away. If he found the perfect place, he'd come back and get rid of the house. It felt good to have a plan, a great relief, in fact, but then he began to hear his dead wife's voice. It started in their bedroom and then moved throughout the house.

She was not happy with his selling *her* home, as she put it, and she made her feelings known in an increasingly belligerent manner, prompting him to wonder if ghosts could also be eliminated by pushing them down the basement stairs.

"DEAR AUTHOR, LET ME EXPLAIN WHY THIS IS TOO MUCH OF A DOWNER FOR OUR PRESS . . ."

He wrote replies with dark messages to publishers who wrote dark messages to him about his stories with dark messages.

Late Stage Parents

Acting was in his blood since he was a small child. Whenever he had a chance to perform, he leapt at it. There was nothing to that point in his short life as gratifying as playing the back end of a donkey, and he made the most of the part by biting the ass of the kid in front of him. For that he was expelled from school and required to meet with a child psychologist before being allowed to return. It was then his parents recognized the extent of their youngster's gift. When he used an actual knife for a stabbing scene in a future play, they were over the stars.

ROADBLOCKS

For most of his adult life Dan had the notion he might one day buy a small piece of property—a spread, as they called it out there on the eastern plains of Colorado. As a kid he'd accompanied his father on business trips from St. Paul to Salt Lake City a couple of times and had fallen under the spell of that part of the country. It spoke to him for reasons he could not quite articulate. All he knew it was a place he wanted to be. Now, at 65, recently retired and widowed, he figured it was the perfect time to follow his instincts. To go to his "happy place," as he'd long thought of it. So, he packed up his house, sold off everything, including the house itself, and prepared to head west. He was excited by the prospect of what may await him in the wide-open spaces. It seemed the first time he was going to have an actual adventure. And then a thought seized him as he climbed into his car. *It's probably going to be lonely as hell out there.*

PANDEMIC

Everybody was losing track of the days. Was it Tuesday? Was it Saturday? Which month was it? It wasn't that people were dying. It was that they did not know when.

Her Plans Were Up in the Air

She'd been on the space station for almost a year and was proud of her accomplishment and service to her country. While she was aloft things began to crumble back on Earth, due to extreme political upheaval and a devastating airborne pathogen. When it came time to return, she decided to remain in place. There was no response when she conveyed her plan to Houston.

Highly Exposed

I was sitting in the kitchen having a bowl of beef barley soup when there was a sudden violent crash just above me. When I looked up I was shocked to see two legs hanging through the ceiling. They belonged to my wife. I had warned her time and again to wear underpants while doing her high jump exercises in her second-floor studio.

Steadfast

There were guns everywhere I looked in my uncle's house, yet my dad's older brother was the nicest person I ever knew. The saying, "He wouldn't kill a flea," described him to a tee. That was before he got hooked on crack cocaine and killed a convenience store clerk for money to get a fix. Even after that, my opinion of him didn't change. Everybody loved him in prison.

Life Goes On

The wind is stronger than we expected at this point in the approaching storm. The weatherman says we're about to get hit by a Category 4 hurricane, so we've taken what precautions we can to save our house and property. Our main concern is the rising river nearby. It will overflow but we're praying it will not breach our property. My husband is pretty certain it will and he's sandbagged as much as he can to prevent flooding in our basement that would ruin our new family room. The big oak is also a major concern, and he's propped it up with two-by-fours and some guy-wire to keep it from toppling on us. I'm still thinking I have time to make a run to TJ's for an outfit I need for next Saturday night's class reunion. The radio just said parts of town have lost power, so I better get going.

DATE NIGHT

The shadows of the tree limbs against her bedroom ceiling played out a scenario in which a saucer-shaped object landed and a six-limbed figure slid down its ramp. When the doorbell rang, she knew what it was and shouted to her mother to let it in.

WHEN TRADITION IS DEFIED

Once a year, young lovers would gather at the summit of Orkhon Falls in Mongolia to express their devotion to one another. It was a centuries old custom and tantamount to a wedding proposal. Nearly all of the couples would marry shortly thereafter. However, that was not the case with Munnokhoi and Bayarmaa, who decided to occupy their newly constructed yurt without formalizing their relationship. This upset their relatives and friends, resulting in no RSVPs for their announced house warming reception.

INFINITE DISAPPOINTMENT

By 2850, humans had explored the far reaches of the universe and discovered that the intelligence level of life forms scattered throughout were nearly identical to their own.

Maturity

Over time Barry grew aware of his limitations, so he wisely avoided things he knew he was not qualified to attempt. This kept him from embarrassing situations, such as when he agreed to debate a nuclear physicist although he had no background in science. Not long after that debacle he realized he should keep his mouth shut. Knowing this made his life better.

Shhh

My wife was the champion of our whisper-fighting. For me to win
arguments, I had to speak at full volume. My victories depended on
the power of my vocal cords. Indeed, I could dominate our debates
with my basso profundo cranked full throttle. My wife would cover
her ears, curse, and run out of the room. Score another for me. It
was a different thing when our four-year-old daughter was put to
bed. She was a light sleeper, and I was disarmed.

Mixed Message

We eat out too much, says my husband. We're retired and on a budget, so we have to watch our money, he says. Then he says you want to catch a bite out tonight.

CAREFUL WHAT YOU WISH FOR

When Carlyle gave a panhandler money after leaving his favorite watering hole, he was told he could make five wishes. He laughed off the stranger's offer and continued on home. Midway there, he began to think what he would ask for if it were actually true. "Okay, let's see, to be 25 years old, very good looking, exceedingly rich, in perfect health, and a pilot," he mumbled. In a flash, he found himself peering admiringly at a young attractive face in the reflection of a private jet's windscreen. Sixty-five years later he lamented the fact he had not wished-for immortality.

THE CAKE MAKER

Jennifer expressed her feelings about the crucial events in her life by making confections that reflected them. When her newest boyfriend left her, she busied herself in the kitchen assembling the ingredients it would require. To her dismay she could not locate the jar of arsenic she'd used for several similar occasions. Had she run out?

CRITICS BE DAMNED

It's easy to make fun of Rod McKuen, but if you try really hard you can actually hear the warm.

BRAVE PAUL

On the hospital bed in the small front room, he rapidly wastes away. This young man . . . this fighter of fire. He smiles courageously and makes jokes to ease his family's concern. He winces from the pain but says he's okay. How dark the long night of the ravaged body. How fraught with hungry ghosts. When the last day comes, he utters characteristic words to those at his side, "I'll get through this," and in the quiet of the next dawn, he does.

Distraction

Leonard Cohen shows an interviewer how he meditates. He sits in the lotus position on a pink wall-to-wall rug in a large empty room in the monk's monastery, where he resides intermittently toward the end of his life. The attractive female interlocutor kneels close to him in a very short skirt. Cohen attempts to avert his eyes from her with varying degrees of success.

PRE-DAWN TEXT FROM AN *OLD* FRIEND

"Chipped a damn tooth on a health bar last night. It has 12 grams of protein and a $200 dental bill as a wellness benefit. I give up. This never happens with jelly donuts."

GUILTY CONSCIENCE

Back in his long-ago history he had violently forced himself on a female classmate. It had not been reported and he never heard from her again. Now, a successful businessman with a good marriage and two teenage children, the assault haunted him. He fervently hoped the young woman had come to an early end so that his crime would not be exposed.

Hearing Voices

I used to walk around being my own radio.
— Robert Stone

The disc jockey in his head did the show especially for him, often telling him he was well-loved and warning him about certain people who might do him harm. Whatever he wanted to hear was played for his benefit and his benefit alone. *I am so lucky to have a radio in my head*, he thought.

READING THE SHEETS

Keira washed the bedclothes at the local home for disabled children. She never actually saw the "clients," as they were called, because the laundry room was in the deep recesses of the maintenance building far from the resident area. Despite this she felt she knew them. The worn and soiled covers revealed many things to her about the physically challenged youngsters. Most of all she could discern their sadness, and when the linens were ready to return to their beds, she would hold them close and whisper tender words hoping the little ones would be soothed by them.

Everything in Its Own Time

I see a seagull fly over a single stack freighter in a 1920s YouTube video and think to myself, *I bet that bird is dead by now.*

FORGIVENESS

The one time she had sex outside of her marriage turned into a fiasco. She'd rendezvoused with an office mate at a nearby Motel 6 after months of furtive ass-grabbing and flirtation. Once in the hotel room, they quickly disrobed and he mounted her. Not a second later he toppled from the bed and split his forehead on the nightstand. Embarrassed, if not humiliated, by the disastrous tryst, she ended her extramarital dalliance. Years later, she confessed her ill-fated affair to her husband, who failed to see, as she did, the humor in the incident. Over time, he would laugh about it with his second wife.

Watching Videos of Dead Writers

Cary enjoyed watching famous authors talk about their craft hoping he'd learn some valuable lessons that would benefit his own writing. When he realized that most were no longer alive, he wondered if he'd wasted his time.

Bedside Manner

His colonoscopy revealed a precancerous polyp and so he was advised to return for another procedure in three years to see if it had turned malignant. Google assured him a very small percentage of these growths became cancer and he breathed easier. Then he was told he should return in one year for another colonoscopy because his polyp was so minute they were not sure they'd completely removed all of it. "It's good that it's so tiny, but it could bloat up like a floating body," observed his gastroenterologist.

Motorcyclist

Who *is* that idiot atop that nasty loud machine? Such a disturbance of the peace. Such an indifference to others. Fuck him and the Harley he road in on.

FOOTSY

He showed her that one of his feet had six toes. She didn't know what to think when she saw it. "Do you have other strange anomalies on your body?" she asked, querulously. When he removed his other sock, she saw he only had four toes on that foot, to which he remarked, "See, on balance, I'm perfectly normal." She wasn't buying it.

THE POLES OF MY DESIRE

Passionate intimacy with my lover at one end. A million miles of space between us at the other.

Go Fish

Randy and his friends charter a fishing boat for the day. The plan is to catch Alaskan halibut, have it filleted, freeze dried, and shipped home to Connecticut. He's never been deep sea fishing and has some reservations about it, but he's still excited about the experience—taken by the romantic notion and adventure of it. The air is crisp but comfortable and the snow-capped volcanos across the inlet are inspiring. The scene is perfect, cinematic. An hour from the dock, the captain says "drop your lines," and the day anglers let the weights carry their hooks away from the slowly moving vessel. Not ten minutes later, Randy's rod bends and his buddies shout, "You got one! Haul it in." He cranks the reel and draws back on the handle with all the force he can muster. "Take it easy. Don't lose it," advises the skipper, moving to his side. After several minutes pulling at the line he's exhausted and thinks he can't hold on to the pole much longer. *I just don't have the upper body strength for this*, he admits to myself. He's saved from certain humiliation when one of the boat's hired hands grabs a gaff and pulls his catch on board. Cheers go up all around, and he feels like Hemingway until he sees the beautiful sea creature squirming and flapping on the deck and gulping for air. Then every molecule of his being wants to scream, *Save it! Throw it back into the water! Don't let it die!*

Later He Wondered If He'd Committed a Mortal Sin

When his prayers went unanswered, he angrily chomped on the Holy Eucharist in Sunday Mass. He'd been warned against it in catechism, Sister Jeanine saying, "Remember, it's the body of Christ. Let the wafer melt on your tongue." Jude had been accused of vindictiveness before.

Michael C. Keith is the author or coauthor of more than two dozen groundbreaking books on electronic media, including one chosen by President Clinton for his official summer reading list. Beyond that, he is the author of an acclaimed memoir, a young adult novel, and 18 story collections—his latest, *Insomnia 11*, is from MadHat Press. He was nominated for a Pushcart Prize several times, a Pen O.Henry Award, and was a finalist for the National Indie Excellence Award for short fiction anthology and a finalist for the 2013 International Book Award in the "Fiction Visionary" category.

Books by Michael C. Keith

Fiction

The Late Epiphany of a Low-Key Oracle (2021) Nixes-Mate Press
Leaning West (2020) Cervena Barva Press
Insomnia 11 (2020) MadHat Press
Stories in the Key of Me (2019) Regal House Publishing
Let Us Now Speak of Extinction (2018) MadHat Press
Perspective Drifts Life a Log on a River (2017) PalmArts Publishing
Slow Transit (2017) Cervena Barva Press
Bits, Specks, Crumbs, Flecks (2016) Vraeyda Literary
Vapors (2017) Big Table Publishing
The Near Enough (2016) Cold River Press
If Things Were Made to Last Forever (2014) Big Table Publishing
Caricatures (2014) Strange Days Books
The Collector of Tears (2014) Underground Voices Books
Everything is Epic (2013) Silver Birch Press
Sad Boy (2013) Big Table Publishing

Of Night and Light (2012) Blue Mustang Press
Hoag's Object (2011) Whiskey Creek Press
And Through the Trembling Air (2010) Blue Mustang Press
Life is Falling Sideways (2009) Parlance Press

Non-Fiction

Norman Corwin's 'One World Flight' (2009) Continuum Books
Radio Cultures: The Sound Medium in American Life (2008) Peter
Lang Publishing
Sounds of Change (2008) University North Carolina Press
The Quieted Voice (2006) Southern Illinois University Press
The Radio Station, 8th ed. (2010) Focal Press
The Broadcast Century and Beyond, 5th ed. (2010) Focal Press
The Next Better Place (2003) Algonquin Books
Dirty Discourse (2003) Iowa University Press
Sounds in the Dark (2001) Iowa State University Press
Queer Airwaves (2001) M.E. Sharpe Publishing
Talking Radio (2000) M.E. Sharpe Publishing
Waves of Rancor (1999) M.E. Sharpe Publishing
The Hidden Screen (1999) M.E. Sharpe Publishing
Voices in the Purple Haze (1997) Praeger Publishing
Global Broadcasting Systems (1996) Focal Press
Signals in the Air (1995) Praeger Publishing
Selling Radio Direct (1992) Focal Press
Radio Programming (1987) Focal Press